QUINT
RIDG.
BIRM.
Loans are
not retu
at the l
3 time
Pleas

The Billionaire's Bidding

BARBARA DUNLOP

MILLS & BOON®

Pure reading pleasure™

All the characters in this book have no existence outside the imagination of the author, and have no relation whatsoever to anyone bearing the same name or names. They are not even distantly inspired by any individual known or unknown to the author, and all the incidents are pure invention.

All Right   luction
in whole   ıblished
by arrang   //S.à.r.l.
The text c   ay
not be rep
by any me   ıg
photocop   on
retrieval s   n
permissic

® and TM are trademarks owned and used by the trademark owner and/or its licensee. Trademarks marked with ® are registered with the United Kingdom Patent Office and/or the Office for Harmonisation in the Internal Market and in other countries.

First published in Great Britain 2008
Large Print edition 2008
Harlequin Mills & Boon Limited,
Eton House, 18-24 Paradise Road,
Richmond, Surrey TW9 1SR

© Barbara Dunlop 2007

ISBN: 978 0 263 20138 3

Set in Times Roman 16¾ on 19 pt.
36-0908-45531

Printed and bound in Great Britain
by Antony Rowe Ltd, Chippenham, Wiltshire

BARBARA DUNLOP

writes romantic stories while curled up in a log cabin in Canada's far north, where bears outnumber people, and it snows six months of the year. Fortunately, she has a brawny husband and two teenage children to haul firewood and clear the driveway while she sips cocoa and muses about her upcoming chapters. Barbara loves to hear from readers. You can contact her through her website at www.barbaradunlop.com.

For my beloved grandmother,
Lucy May Mallory.

One

Emma McKinley should have been nervous as she stepped off the elevator onto the Garrison Hotels' corporate floor. But her emotions had been wrung dry days ago.

It all started with her father's sudden death. Then she discovered McKinley Inns' massive debts. And then she learned of the bizarre financial offer made to her sister in order to save the family corporation.

The only thing left inside her now was a grim determination. And it was focused on Alex Garrison, the CEO of Garrison Hotels.

She clamped her bag against her Donna Karan

blazer and marched her matching pumps straight down the marble-pillared hallway. She'd never been in the Garrison offices before, never had a reason to talk to her family's rivals. But it didn't take a genius to figure out the double doors at the far end would lead to Alex Garrison's inner sanctum.

She ignored the stares from admin staff whose desks were tucked into discreet alcoves along the way. Nobody seemed inclined to stop her. Just as well, she wasn't in a mood to be stopped. She might not have an appointment with Mr. Garrison, but she had a moral right to confront him in person.

How dare he take advantage of her little sister, Katie, mere weeks after the funeral, with his veiled threats and outrageous propositions?

Emma drew a breath into her tightening lungs.

Maybe she did have some emotion left in her after all.

"Excuse me, ma'am," came a female voice on her left as the hallway widened into a posh reception area.

Emma didn't answer. She didn't glance across the desk at the woman, and she didn't break stride. Ten feet from his door. Eight feet.

"Ma'am." The voice was louder this time, more strident as a neatly suited, thirty-something woman jumped up from her chair.

Five feet.

"You can't go—"

Emma clamped her hand around the elongated, ornate gold door handle.

"—*in there.*"

Emma swung the door wide open.

Four men in dark suits, sitting at a round, mahogany meeting table, turned sharply to stare at her. Two were gray-haired, with bushy eyebrows and accusatory squints that told her she'd made a terrible blunder. The third was a younger, blond man. His sparkling blue eyes and restrained grin told her he welcomed the interruption.

The fourth man shot to his feet, pushing a leather chair backward with the motion. Dark-haired, dark-eyed and broad-shouldered, his stance told her he was more than ready to take on her and anybody else who breached his privacy.

"I'm so sorry, Mr. Garrison," came the secretary's breathless voice from behind Emma. "I tried—"

"Not your fault, Simone." The man's slate-gray gaze never left Emma. "Can I help you with something?"

Emma's grip tightened on her shoulder bag. Everyone else in the room faded to mist as her anger returned in force. She focused on Alex Garrison. "Did you think there was the *slightest* chance I'd let you get away with it?"

Simone gasped.

"As you can see." Alex's jaw clenched over the steel-threaded words. "We're in the middle of a meeting."

"I don't care if you're—"

"If you'd like to make an appointment."

"I would not."

"Then I'll have to ask you to leave."

"Do you know who I am?"

"No."

"Liar."

"I'll call security," said Simone.

Alex raised his eyebrows, gazing blandly back at Emma. She realized with a jolt that he really didn't know who she was. How was that possible? Katie was the public face of McKinley Inns, sure. But...

"Do we *need* security?" he asked.

"I'm Emma McKinley."

His nostrils flared and he jerked back ever so slightly.

Then, after a silent pause, he lifted a gold pen from the tabletop and tucked it into the breast pocket of his finely tailored jacket. His burgundy silk tie gleamed under the discreet lighting as he straightened to full height. "If you'll excuse us, gentlemen. I believe I can spare five minutes for Ms. McKinley."

The men started to rise.

Alex held up a broad hand. "Please. Ms. McKinley and I will use the boardroom."

He gestured to a wide oak door and indicated she should precede him.

She crossed the room and turned yet another ornate gold handle. The doorway opened into an impressively large boardroom, dominated by an oblong table of polished, inlayed wood. The twenty chairs surrounding it were covered in burgundy leather, and a bank of windows running down one side let in the August sun that was hanging over uptown Manhattan.

She heard the door click shut, and she pivoted to face him.

"I trust you can make this quick," he said, taking a single step toward her, planting his oxfords wide apart.

He was even larger and more impressive up close, with broad shoulders and a deep, muscular chest. Stark sunrays highlighted the uncompromising planes of his face. His chin was square, the set of his lips grim, and his eyes were the color of gunmetal gray after a glistening rain.

She got the feeling few people crossed him and lived to tell the tale. If she didn't know he'd been born with a silver spoon in his mouth, she'd swear he grew up on the streets of Brooklyn.

Not that any of it mattered. He wasn't getting his hands on her baby sister or their company.

"You are *not* marrying Katie," she stated bluntly.

He gave a careless shrug. "I believe that's up to Katie."

"My father isn't even cold in his grave."

"Doesn't change your financial situation."

"I can fix our financial situation." Maybe.

Hopefully. They could always mortgage the Martha's Vineyard property.

Alex cocked his head to one side. "I can have your loan called within twenty-four hours. Can you fix your finances that fast?"

Emma didn't answer. He knew darn well she couldn't fix them that fast. It would take weeks, maybe months to work through the maze of mortgages, letters of credit and personal guarantees signed by her father.

Her chest tingled and tightened. Why, oh, why did her father have to die so young? She missed him desperately. And she'd counted on having his guidance for decades to come.

"Ms. McKinley?"

"Why do you even *want* McKinley Inns?"

Garrison Hotels had dozens of properties, bigger, more opulent facilities. McKinley occupied a small, high-end niche, where Garrison could compete with any luxury hotel chain in the world.

"You're joking, right?"

She shook her head.

"Like anyone, I want to expand. And you're an opportunity."

"And you don't care who gets trampled in the process?"

The man's reputation was well and truly deserved. Though his press coverage had become more flattering over the past months, Emma wasn't fooled. He was a coldhearted takeover artist who profited from other people's misfortune.

He took another step forward and crossed his arms over his chest. "I don't think Katie made the situation clear. I'm the one doing *you* a favor."

Emma's spine snapped straight. She tipped her chin to look him in the eyes. "By marrying my sister and taking over our company?"

"By saving your company from bankruptcy. You're insolvent, Ms. McKinley. If I don't take you out, somebody else will. That's the way capitalism works."

"Don't patronize me."

A cold grin flexed one side of his mouth. "Way I see it, this is a win-win."

"The way *I* see it, this is a lose-lose."

"That's because you're idealistic and impractical."

"At least I have a soul."

He shifted his stance. "Last time I checked, a soul wasn't a requirement for a business license in the state of New York."

"She will *not* marry you."

"Did she explain the deal?"

Yes, Katie had explained the deal. Alex wanted their company. But he'd spent thousands of dollars over the last two years improving his image, and he was afraid of negative publicity from preying on two newly bereaved sisters.

Oh, he still wanted to prey on them. He just didn't want anybody to know about it. Hence the cover of marriage and all the joyous goodwill that would go with it.

"She told me," said Emma tightly.

"Then you know you'll keep half the company." His impassive expression turned to a scowl. "And I'm crazy for offering you that much."

"You actually expect to buy a bride."

"At that price. Yeah."

Emma honestly didn't know what to say.

"Are we done?" he asked.

Were they done? What did she do now? Make a hollow threat? Storm out the door? Swear he'd never get his hands on her precious inns when they both knew that's exactly what he would do?

He seemed to sense her hesitation. "Nobody gets hurt," he said. "The publicity will help us both. The press will go nuts over the merging of two great hotel families. We'll feed the story to female reporters, who'll get all misty-eyed at—"

She raked her bangs back from her forehead. "Are you *listening* to yourself?"

He blinked. "What do you mean?"

"You don't find that plan just a little cold-blooded?"

"Like I said, nobody gets hurt."

"What about Katie? What about David?"

"Who's David?"

"Her boyfriend. The sweet, gentle caring young man she's been dating for six months. He'll be heartbroken and humiliated."

Alex paused. For a second she thought she saw an actual emotion pass through his eyes. But then it was gone, replaced by hard gloss slate once again. "David will get over it. He can marry her later, when she's worth a lot more money."

Emma opened her mouth, but no sound came out.

"What about you?" Alex asked into the silence.

"I'm pretty upset," she answered, in the understatement of the century.

He rolled his eyes. "Your emotional state is irrelevant. Do you have a steady boyfriend?"

"*No.*" And what did that have to do with anything?

"Problem solved."

"Huh?"

"You marry me."

Emma reached out to grip the back of a leather chair, afraid she might lose it right there. "What?"

Alex stood there, looking for all the world like a rational person, while tossing out the most outrageous proposal she'd heard in her life. Marry him? *Marry* him?

"It doesn't really matter which sister," he continued without a thread of emotion in his voice. "I only picked Katie because she's—"

"The pretty one," Emma finished, straightening away from the chair and squaring her shoulders. For some reason it killed her to have him of all people say it out loud. Not that everybody didn't think it. It was just that Alex cut to the heart of the issue with such dispassionate accuracy, that it hurt more than usual.

"That's not—"

"I am not marrying you, and Katie is not marrying you."

Alex's voice took on a soft warning note. "Option three is calling your loan. Then you get nothing."

Emma tightened her arm on her shoulder bag. "Option three is me working out the finances first thing tomorrow morning."

His mouth crooked in another half smile. "In that case, I'll leave my offer open for twenty-four hours."

She turned and stalked toward a side door. Her exit was all bluff and bravado, and they both knew it. For that alone, she'd never forgive him.

"No need, Mr. Garrison," she said tightly.

"Under the circumstances," he rumbled behind her, as she reached for the handle and twisted.

"You might want to call me Alex…Emma."

She didn't turn back, but her name on his lips sent a shiver up her spine.

* * *

Two hours later, the office door closed behind the Rockwell brothers, and Ryan Hayes turned his stare on Alex. "I assume you nailed down the details with her?"

Alex closed the top manila folder, carefully straightening the pile on the polished tabletop in front of him. "Not quite."

Ryan narrowed his gaze. "What do you mean not quite?"

Alex sighed and leaned back in his chair, rubbing a fingertip across his temple. Gunter's plan was looking more ridiculous by the minute. "I mean, the details aren't nailed down yet."

"But you are getting married."

"I'm trying," Alex snapped.

Ryan shook an admonishing finger. "You are not touching McKinley Inns without a bona fide McKinley bride on your arm. Jeez, Alex, they'll crucify us in the press."

Alex gritted his teeth. He'd turned this thing over in his mind a thousand different ways. If it was up to him, he'd call the loan right now and take over the damn company. This was business, not a day care for dilettantes.

But Ryan and Gunter were both major share-holders in Garrison Hotels. And they were both convinced that Alex's reputation as a hard-ass was hurting business. They even thought some recent, decisive takeover bids had harmed employee morale and impacted on convention business.

As a result, they were forcing him to behave like a boy scout in public. He wasn't allowed to argue, wasn't even allowed to scowl. Soon they'd have him kissing babies and helping little old ladies across the street.

"Why don't *you* marry her?" he asked Ryan.

"Because I'm not the one with the image problem," Ryan countered. "Besides, I'm not the CEO, and I'm not the public face of Garrison Hotels. Profits were up fifteen percent for the quarter."

Alex glanced at his watch. "That could've been anything." He wasn't ready to accept that the kinder, gentler Alex was responsible for such an enormous turnaround.

"So what are the details?" asked Ryan.

Alex looked up. "Huh?"

"What's left to sort out with Katie."

"Nothing. It's not Katie. It's Emma now. And she's still making up her mind." Alex couldn't believe he'd proposed to two different women in the space of forty-eight hours.

Ryan cocked his head. "I thought you proposed to the pretty one."

"The pretty one said no. So I proposed to Emma instead. *She* doesn't have a boyfriend."

"I guess not," Ryan scoffed.

Alex's spine stiffened. Sure, Emma wasn't a knockout like Katie, but there was no need to get insulting. "What's that supposed to mean?"

"It means she's tough and scary."

Alex stood up. "Wimp."

Emma wasn't tough and scary. She was frustrated and panicking. Which worked in his favor, actually.

Ryan stood with him. "One sister or the other. You make this work or bail on the project."

Bail on the project? Alex didn't think so. McKinley had prime beachfront property on Kayven Island. Prime beachfront property whose value was *about* to go through the roof when the cruise ship facility was finally announced.

He might have to sweeten the deal or find

another vulnerability to exploit. But he wasn't walking away from this one.

"What are we going to *do?*" Katie's face was pale as she leaned across the table at the Chateau Moulin restaurant off the lobby of the McKinley Inn Fifth Avenue. The flickering hurricane lamp emphasized her worry, reflecting in a window that was blackened by the park beyond.

"I don't know," Emma answered honestly with a shake of her head. "I'll have to call the bank in the morning."

"And tell them *what?*" Katie's voice rose to high C, matching the note of a grand piano tinkling in the corner.

"We'll restructure the mortgages, maybe use the Martha's Vineyard property as extra collateral."

"You know that won't work."

Emma didn't answer, because Katie was right. Equity in the Martha's Vineyards property wouldn't make a dent in the amount their father owed.

Things had been tough for McKinley the past few years. Bookings were down, costs up. Their father was always reluctant to let staff go. And they were locked into major renovations on three ski resort properties, while snow conditions had remained poor two winters in a row.

They were over a barrel, and Alex Garrison knew it. The man might be amoral, but he wasn't stupid.

"I'm going to have to marry him," said Katie, raising her palms in a gesture of defeat.

"And what about David?"

"I'll explain it to him somehow."

Emma took a drink from her martini glass, mimicking her sister's voice. "I'm so sorry, sweetheart. But I'm going to have to marry another man for his money."

"I won't say it like that."

"There's no way to say it and make it sound good."

"Well, are *you* going to marry him?"

Emma didn't answer as the waitress set salads in front of them.

"At least I don't have a boyfriend," she hissed, after the waitress left.

Katie straightened, looking tragically hopeful. "Is that a yes?"

"No, it's not a yes." Then Emma paused, desperately trying to gather her thoughts. "We can't…" She clenched her jaw. "It's not right… It *galls* me to even think about giving in to that man."

"At least we'd keep half the company."

Fair point. Emma took another sip of her drink. If Alex got the bank to call in the loan instead, they'd be lucky to keep one hotel.

If only they had more time. If only they knew someone who could underwrite them quickly and extensively. If only their father's heart hadn't given out.

The three of them were a team. They'd weathered storms before, and she was sure they could have found a way out of this maze.

"Emma?" Katie prompted.

Emma picked up her fork and stabbed into the shrimp salad. "We'll need to talk to Legal."

Katie's blue eyes dimmed in the lamplight. "To declare bankruptcy."

Emma drew a bracing breath. No. They weren't declaring bankruptcy. Not when they had a slightly more palatable choice.

They were going to throw their lot in with

Alex Garrison. If they didn't, they'd be out on the street, and he'd be undermining their father's life's work by this time tomorrow.

At least with Alex there was a chance. If they had a few good years, maybe they could buy him out.

And it wasn't like Emma had a boyfriend waiting anywhere in the wings. Nor was she likely to have one in the foreseeable future. Plain-looking, plainspoken hotel executives who traveled half the year weren't exactly hot prospects on dating dot com.

Truth was, a marriage on paper wouldn't be that big of an inconvenience for her. A justice of the peace, a couple of publicity snapshots, and they'd barely have to see each other again.

She looked Katie straight in the eyes, not giving herself time to rethink the decision. "We have to talk to Legal so we can make sure Alex can't do something crazy with our inns."

Katie's eyes went wide. "You're going to do it?"

Emma dropped her fork and drained her glass. "I'm going to do it."

Two

Mrs. Nash had been calling Alex *Alex* his entire life. But since he'd moved out of his penthouse and back into the family's Long Island mansion six months ago—another of Ryan's brilliant plans to improve his image—she'd taken to calling him Mr. Garrison. Every time she did it, Alex glanced around for his father.

The old man might have been dead for three years, but he still had the power to make Alex jump. It was bad enough that Alex had taken over his father's study, he didn't need to take on his name as well.

"Call me Alex," he grumbled, glancing up from the financial section.

Mrs. Nash squared her shoulders in the doorway. "*Mr.* Garrison." Her faint British accent grew more pronounced when she was annoyed. "A Ms. McKinley has arrived to see you."

Alex flipped his newspaper down at the fold, his senses coming on alert. "Which one?"

Mrs. Nash's formidable brow went up. "Ms. Emma McKinley, *sir.*"

"Okay, now you're just trying annoy me."

"Sir?" There was an undeniable twinkle behind her blue-gray eyes.

"It's Alex. *Alex.* You changed my diapers and smacked my butt."

She sniffed. "And I dare say, it didn't help much, did it now?"

Alex set the newspaper on his spotless, mahogany desktop and stood from the tufted leather wing chair. "Can we at least dispense with the sir?"

"Yes, Mr. Garrison."

He drew closer to her as he headed for the door. "You're fired."

Her expression remained impassive. "I think not."

"Because you know where the bodies are buried?"

"Because *you've* never memorized the combination to the wine cellar."

He paused. "Excellent point."

"Very good then…sir."

"Insubordinate," he muttered as he passed her.

"Will Ms. McKinley be staying to lunch?"

Good question. Was Emma going to say yes and make both their lives easier? Or was she going to stay up there on her high horse and cause him no end of trouble? Alex gave it a fifty-fifty chance.

He drew a bracing breath. "I have no idea."

Mrs. Nash nodded and carried on into the study, where she'd straighten the newspaper and erase any lingering trace of his presence. It was eerie, living in a house that forgot about you every time you left the room. Sometimes he'd leave subtle traces, a book out of place on a bookshelf, a sculpture slightly to the left on the mantel. But he hadn't tripped her up yet.

He headed down the hallway under the watchful eyes of his ancestors. The portraits were newly dusted and plum-line straight. His father was last, looking dour and judgmental, probably wishing he could grill Alex on the bottom line. Alex imagined that's what his father hated most about being dead—standing by silently while Alex ran amok with the family business.

He rounded the corner to see his latest business problem standing in the sky-lit rotunda foyer, clutching a patterned handbag against an ivory, tailored coatdress. Her shoulder-length, chestnut hair was tucked behind her ears and pulled sleek by a pair of sunglasses perched atop her head. Her lashes were dark against coffee-toned eyes, her lips were shaded a lustrous pink, and diamond studs twinkled against her earlobes. She was immaculately made-up and clearly nervous.

That could be a good sign, or it could be a bad sign.

"Emma." Alex held out his hand, deciding to pretend they hadn't parted on sarcastic terms.

"Alex," she nodded with a brief, brusque shake.

"Would you care to come in?" he asked, gesturing toward the hallway.

She peered suspiciously down the wide corridor.

"To my study," he elaborated. "We might be more comfortable there."

After a second's hesitation, Emma nodded. "All right. Thanks."

"Not a problem." He waited until she was beside him, then fell into step.

"How was traffic?" he asked, instantly regretting the impulse to make small talk. He wasn't nervous. He was cool as a cucumber when it came to business deals. And this one was no different than any other.

If she said no, she said no. He'd either change her mind or come up with plan B. Ryan was making way too much of this wedding thing, anyway. Alex's future didn't depend on Ms. McKinley's whims.

His study was back to being immaculate, as he knew it would be. The newspaper had been folded and placed in the front center of the desk. Alex knew he should sit behind it, putting himself in a position of power. But instead he touched one of the wing chairs clustered around the stone fireplace, gesturing for Emma to sit down.

She nodded her thanks, sinking into the chair and crossing one shapely leg over the other. She smoothed her ivory skirt and tucked the frivolous handbag in beside her.

Then she folded both her hands over her slender knees and looked up.

He quickly cleared his head of the picture her legs made and sat down across from her.

"Traffic was fine," she said.

He nodded, telling himself to get straight down to business. "And you've made up your mind?"

She drew back ever so slightly. Then she nodded. "Yes. I have."

He cocked his head. "And?"

She twisted a sapphire-and-emerald band around her right ring finger. "I'll marry you."

She sounded like she was agreeing to the gallows.

Well, it wasn't going to be any picnic for him either. He was about to saddle himself with a reluctant wife, curtailing his social life, curtailing his sex life and, given her current expression and body language, conjugal relations weren't going to be any part of this union.

Which meant he was celibate. For the duration. Wasn't that just wonderful.

"Thank you," he forced out.

She gave a sharp nod and made to rise.

"Wait."

She arched a brow.

"You don't think we have more to discuss?"

"What's to discuss?" she asked. But she did sit back in the chair and recross her legs.

"For starters, who do you *absolutely* have to tell?"

"That I'm marrying you?"

He shook his head. "That it's a fake."

"Oh."

"Yeah. That part. My business partners know."

"My sister knows."

"Anyone else?"

"My lawyer." It was her turn to sit forward. "You can expect a call from him on the prenup."

Alex coughed out a laugh. "You want a prenup?"

"Of course."

"You check my net worth in *Forbes* last year?" A prenup protected him a whole lot more than it protected her.

The expression in her brown eyes was more than a little judgmental. "Of course not. I couldn't care less about your net worth."

He found that somewhat hard to believe. But, whatever. The important thing was to get this farce moving along. "First thing we have to do is get engaged."

"I thought we just did that."

He opened his mouth, but she kept talking.

"You said 'marry me or I'll bankrupt you.' And I decided to take the lesser of two evils." Her pretty lips pursed. "And, you know, I really don't think it gets any more romantic than that."

Sarcasm? She was getting millions of dollars, while he was accepting an inferior business deal for the sake of his reputation, and she was handing out sass?

"You're not very grateful, are you?" he asked.

"Your blackmail victims are usually grateful?"

He shook his head in disbelief. So much for Emma being panicked and intimidated. "You were expecting champagne and flowers?"

"I was hoping for a bank loan and a good actuary."

"Well, you got me instead."

She nodded slowly, peering down her delicate nose at him. "That I did."

This bickering wasn't getting them anywhere.

Alex stood, shaking off his restless energy. "If we're going to make this work, there are a few things we'll have to do up front."

"Like learn to tolerate each other?"

"Like convince the press we're in love."

Emma's lips slowly curved into a grin. First time he'd actually seen her smile. It gave her eyes a golden glow and put a dimple in her right cheek. And when the tip of her tongue touched her front teeth, he felt a jolt of desire right down to his toes.

At this rate, he was going to have to rethink which sister was the pretty one.

"What?" he asked, tamping down the unwarranted reaction.

"I've now figured out the difference between us."

Alex squinted. Had he missed something?

"I'm firmly grounded in reality, while you dare to dream the impossible."

He wouldn't have put it quite that way, but true enough.

"I think we can probably learn to tolerate each other," she continued. "I don't see how we could convince anyone we're in love."

Alex took a pace forward, catching the scent

of her perfume, tamping down yet another jolt of desire. This was crazy. He couldn't be attracted to Emma. He wouldn't *let* himself be attracted to Emma.

"You know your biggest problem?" he asked.

She stood up, but he still had eight inches on her. "No, but I bet you're going to tell me."

"It's your defeatist attitude."

"Actually, my biggest problem is you."

"Sweetheart, I am your salvation."

"Humble, aren't we?"

"When you work hard and pay attention, you don't need to be humble." He inched closer, dropping his voice. "There are only six people in the world who know I'm not in love with you. I'm about to convince the rest."

"The *entire* world?" She arched a sassy brow.

"You need to think big, Emma."

"You need to think realistically, Alex."

"They're not mutually exclusive."

"Statistically? I believe they are."

"Then you need to be the exception." Alex grinned to himself. He could give back as much sass as he got. "And, Emma, *my darling,* I am exceptional."

She eloquently rolled her eyes. "Can I get something in the prenup prohibiting your ego?"

"Only if your lawyer's a whole lot better than mine."

She took a half pace back. "So that's your big plan? We gaze adoringly at each other in public, while our lawyers duke it out in the back room?"

He gestured for her to sit back down. "That pretty much covers it. Now, back to our engagement."

She sat down and her chest rose and fell beneath the tailored dress. "I assume we're talking about a very ostentatious ring?"

"Absolutely." He eased down into his own chair. He'd been giving this some thought. In the event, of course, that one of them said yes. "Thing is, we don't want them talking about *if* we're engaged. We want them talking about *how* we got engaged."

Emma paused. "I'm not going to like this, am I?"

"You a Yankees fan?"

She shook her head, and he could see the exact second she got his point.

Her brown eyes went round, and her complexion paled a shade. "No. Oh, no. Not the *JumboTron.*"

"It'd make a splash."

"I'd have to kill you."

"Bad plan. You wouldn't be in my will yet."

"You may not have noticed, but Katie does the McKinley publicity. She's the extrovert."

"If you'll recall, I *did* try to marry Katie."

Emma's expression tightened for a split second, and he realized his words might have sounded like an insult.

"She's taken," Emma declared. "Deal with it."

"I didn't mean—"

"Sure you did. No JumboTron. Got it?"

Alex hadn't meant he preferred Katie. He didn't care one way or the other. But another denial would be overkill. And it would probably just tick Emma off.

"How about if I surprise you?" he asked instead. "Add a bit of realism to the situation."

"This is silly," said Emma, straightening in her chair and getting all prim and proper on him. "We should be talking about the business merger. Who cares how we get engaged?"

Had she missed his point entirely? This whole thing was all about his reputation and his image.

"I care," he stated flatly. Sass was one thing, but she needed to understand his interests. "You're getting one sweetheart of a monetary deal, and I'm getting some good PR. The *how* matters. The *ruse* matters."

She opened her mouth to rebut, but he was done debating.

"Make no mistake about it, Emma. You and I are going to convince the world we've fallen in love or die trying."

"I don't know how I'm going to do it," Emma said to Katie as they walked off court number twelve at Club Connecticut. Distracted by Alex's plan, she'd lost decisively to her sister, game, set and match.

She wasn't an actress. And she wasn't a public person. While some hotel socialites hit the club scene and made the front pages of the tabloid press, Emma jealously guarded her privacy.

"Is he being a real jerk?" asked Katie, sympathy in her voice as she gestured to an empty umbrella table with four white deck chairs.

"No jerkier than we expected," said Emma honestly. "Problem is, he's got this whole fantasy, fool-the-press thing planned. And I'm definitely not up for playing the simpering Wall Street bride."

Katie frowned for a minute as she took her seat. "Well, I suppose he has to get something out of it."

"He's getting our hotels."

"Only half."

Emma raised her eyebrows at her sister. Did Katie honestly think Alex was being reasonable? "We promised him a wife, not a trophy bride for the front page."

Katie shrugged. "So he wants to show you off a little. Why not go with the flow?"

Emma peeled off her sweatband and shook out her hair. "Because the flow will be trite and embarrassing. And, if you'll recall, the flow is also one very big lie."

Katie smirked. "No harm in looking good while you're lying."

Emma pulled a bottle of water out of the acrylic ice bucket in the center of the table. "Quit laughing at me."

"I'm sorry. It's just—"

"That it's me and not you?"

Katie's tone changed. "Of course not. I'm grateful. You know I'm grateful."

Emma sighed. "I have to find a way to convince him to keep this low-key. A justice of the peace. A small announcement in the classified section."

Katie reached for a bottle of water, cracking the cap. "Or I could lend you some clothes and you could hit the party circuit on his arm."

"You're not helping."

"Wouldn't hurt you to get out and about. You know you work too hard."

"Not hard enough to save the company."

"Hey, you're saving the company now."

Emma sat back in her chair. She wasn't saving the company through her guile and business acumen, that was for sure. "It feels like prostitution."

"Without the sex?"

"Without the sex."

"Then it's not prostitution, is it? Lighten up, Emma. We'll go to Saks."

"Oh, yeah. Saks will solve the problem."

Because as long as Emma had the right wardrobe, she could easily prance through uptown Manhattan casting mooning looks in Alex's direction.

She shuddered.

"Oh my," Katie muttered, her attention shifting to a spot over Emma's shoulder.

"Oh my, what?"

"He's here."

"Who's here?" Emma twisted her neck, trying to get a look.

"Alex," said Katie.

Emma froze. *"What?"*

"Alex is here."

She turned to face Katie. "He's not a member."

"Maybe not."

"It's a private club."

"Like the desk clerk's going to tell Alex Garrison he can't have a day pass."

Emma's chest tightened to a tingle. "What's he doing?"

"Coming this way."

"No."

Katie nodded. "Yes." Then she smiled broadly. "Hello, Alex."

Emma felt a warm palm come to rest on her bare, sweaty shoulder. Her muscles hummed beneath the touch, jumping to some bizarre rhythm. Like she'd never been touched by a man before.

She resisted the urge to shrug him off.

"Hi, sweetheart," Alex's voice rumbled in her ear.

Then his lips branded her temple, and the breath whooshed right out of her body. In fact, it was a light, insubstantial touch, but it jump-started her pulse and sent her nerve endings into a frenzy.

She had to tell herself in no uncertain terms to *calm the heck down.*

Giving her shoulder a final squeeze, he eased his big body into the vacant chair next to her and casually helped himself to a bottle of water. "So, how was the game?"

He was wearing a white polo shirt with a single blue stripe over one shoulder. The open collar showed off his strong neck and tanned skin, while the knit weave delineated his broad shoulders and well-defined pecs.

When Emma didn't answer, he raised a dark brow in her direction.

"Fine," she ground out. Now that she was starting to recover, her anger was bubbling up. A kiss at Club Connecticut was almost as bad as the JumboTron. And Alex knew it. The stares from the surrounding table were penetrating.

He nodded easily. "Good."

"I took her in straight sets," said Katie, her tone far too friendly for Emma's liking.

Emma leaned closer to Alex. "I thought we were going to *talk* about this?" she hissed.

He draped an arm casually over the back of her chair. "I'm through talking," he said.

"Well, I'm not."

"Really? That's unfortunate." He glanced around. "Because I think it's too late."

"Cheat," Emma muttered, knowing he'd won through brute force. At least a dozen people had seen that *oh so calculated* kiss.

Alex laughed. Then he raised his voice and looked at Katie. "Congratulations on the win."

Katie grinned in return. "Emma seemed to be having trouble concentrating this morning."

"Really?" Alex gave her shoulder another annoying squeeze, and her body responded with another annoying crackle. She didn't like it. She refused to like it. It had to be revulsion, because it couldn't be anything else.

"Have anything to do with last night?" he asked her loud and clear.

Two tables away, Marion Thurston's stenciled eyebrows shot to her dyed hairline. It seemed to take the woman a moment to gather her wits, but then she reached for a cell phone and hit a speed dial button. It didn't take a rocket scientist to figure out who she'd called. It was a very poorly kept secret that Marion Thurston fed stories to society columnist Leanne Height.

Emma leaned close to Alex again. "I am definitely going to kill you."

"You're still not in the will."

"I no longer care."

Alex laughed again. "Are you busy tomorrow night?" He looked at Katie. "You, too. I booked a table for the Teddybear Trust casino event."

"I don't gamble," said Emma.

"Well, it's time you learned," he said easily.

"I'm in," said Katie. "Is there room for David?"

"Ahhh. The elusive David."

"I don't want to learn," Emma grumbled.

"Blackjack," said Alex. "I'll bankroll you."

"You're not going to—"

His voice turned steely. "I'll bankroll you."

"Fine. You want to put a tattoo on my forehead while you're at it?"

He lifted her hand for a fleeting kiss, his gentle voice at odds with the steely look in his eyes. "No. Just a diamond on your finger."

"We've got trouble on the wedding front," said Ryan, plunking down in a guest chair in Alex's office.

Alex looked up from the McKinley Inns prospectus. "What kind of trouble?"

"The kind that starts with one archrival DreamLodge and ends with Kayven Island."

An adrenaline shot hit Alex's system. "Old man Murdoch knows about Kayven?"

"He has to," said Ryan, sitting forward in the leather chair. "There's no other explanation."

Dread crept through Alex's system. "For what?"

"He's putting together a bid for McKinley."

"Son of a bitch." Alex rocked to his feet, the possibilities winging through his mind. "The whole chain?"

Ryan stood with him. "Just the Kayven property."

Alex closed his eyes for a split second, wrapping his hand around the back of his neck and squeezing hard. "And the women would keep the rest?" It was a dream come true for Emma.

"Yeah," said Ryan.

"How long've we got?"

"He's presenting the offer start of business Monday."

"Who's your source?"

"Adam down in accounting mentioned that his brother-in-law over at Williamson Smythe was looking at the same geologicals as we were."

"He put it together from *that?*"

Ryan shook his head. "Adam doesn't know a thing. I pieced it together myself from six different sources. We're still the only player with the big picture."

Alex's mind clicked through potential scenarios. All of them ended with a DreamLodge win and a Garrison loss. "I can't let him make that offer."

Ryan nodded.

Alex had to shut Murdoch down. So how did he shut Murdoch down before Monday morning? Marry Emma was the obvious answer. "I wonder how she feels about Vegas…."

"You can't marry Emma in the next forty-eight hours."

Alex snorted. "The jet's at JFK—I could marry her in less than five."

"You don't think a quickie Vegas wedding would look *slightly* opportunistic?"

Alex's voice rose. "I'd rather look opportunistic than screw the whole deal."

"And what happens when Murdoch talks to her?"

"By the time Murdoch talks to her, she'll be Mrs. Alex Garrison."

Ryan shook his head. "Not good enough. We don't want Murdoch talking to her at all."

"We can't stop him from talking to her." It was a free country, and DreamLodge owned as many communication devices as anybody else.

Ryan eased back down in his chair, resting

one ankle on the opposite knee. "We can if he thinks there's no point in talking to her."

"There are hundreds of millions at stake."

"Yeah," Ryan agreed quietly. "And we're going to make him think it's all ours."

Alex recognized the cunning gleam in Ryan's eyes. A renewed calm came over him, and he took his seat behind the desk, picking up a gold pen to twirl between his fingertips. "How?"

"We need four things," said Ryan.

Alex was all ears. There was a reason he'd taken Ryan on as a partner. The man was a strategic genius.

"McKinley's financial statements," said Ryan. "Some serious intel on DreamLodge, a quick and dirty marketing mock-up, and a diamond ring on Emma McKinley's finger."

Alex could take care of the ring and the marketing plan. He supposed he could come up with some kind of rational explanation for wanting Emma's financial statements over the weekend. But he didn't have a single contact at DreamLodge. "What kind of intel?"

Ryan hesitated for a single beat. "Can you call Nathaniel?"

Alex blinked at the sound of his cousin's name. "That's a pretty big gun."

"There are hundreds of millions at stake."

Right. Nathaniel it was.

Three

Emma slipped a thick, white McKinley-crested robe over her damp body, slipping on her glasses and flicking back a wisp of hair that had escaped from her clip. The hot tub motor whirred softly in the background as she padded across the penthouse from her bedroom to the living area.

She'd long since gotten past the strangeness of living in a hotel. Now she just enjoyed the view, the expert cleaning service and the convenience of hot meals at any hour of the day or night. McKinley's head offices were on the third floor of the Fifth Avenue Inn. So on blustery winter days, she was only an elevator ride from work.

She pushed the on button on the television remote and curled up in one corner of the wine-colored sectional sofa, tossing a brocade pillow out of the way. It was eleven-fifteen, Friday night. She'd skipped dinner, and she was thinking a cheese tray and a glass of Cabernet would go well with *Business Week Wrap-up* on ANN.

She called an order in to the concierge, then settled back to watch Marvin Coventry interview the CEO of Mediterranean Energy. The company was under scrutiny following a merger with a British company and an alleged payout to a UN envoy's nephew.

A knock sounded a few minutes into the interview, and Emma watched over her shoulder as she headed for the door to let in Korissa.

"Did they remember to add extra grapes?" she asked, while the CEO squirmed under the reporter's questions. Good. His shareholders deserved an explanation.

"I have no idea," came a male voice.

Emma twisted her head to come face to face with Alex Garrison. Her eyes went wide, and she jerked the lapels of her robe together. "I thought you were Korissa."

"I'm Alex." His gaze took in her robe, her haphazard hair and her clunky glasses.

"What are you *doing* here?" She hadn't expected to see him again until tomorrow night at the Teddybear Trust fundraiser, and she definitely wasn't ready to go another round with him. She tugged at her lapels, especially not dressed like this.

He glanced down at the briefcase in his left hand. "I thought you'd like to see my financial records."

"At eleven-thirty at *night?*"

"You said you wanted a prenup."

Sure she wanted a prenup. But not *now*. Right now she wanted to sleep, and to regroup before facing him again. "I'm not—"

"No time like the present." He glanced pointedly at the room behind her, then shifted almost imperceptibly forward.

Emma stepped sideways to block his path as the nearly soundless whirr of a room service cart announced Korissa's arrival.

The woman halted her brisk steps and glanced questioningly at Alex. "Shall I bring another glass?"

"That would be nice," said Alex. And before Emma could protest, he slipped through the door beside her.

Emma wasn't about to make a scene in front of Korissa, but the man was *not* staying. She moved out of the way of the cart.

"Nice," Alex murmured, glancing around at the Persian carpet, the marble fireplace and the Tiffany chandelier.

"Thank you," Emma said stiffly, while Korissa transferred the cheese tray, wine and fresh flowers to the dining table.

Then Korissa left the penthouse and closed the door behind her.

Emma yanked the sash of her robe tight. "This is not a convenient time."

He set the briefcase down on the dining table and held up his palms in surrender. "I apologize. But I just got out of a meeting."

His gaze seemed to snag on her outfit once again.

"I take it you had a free evening?"

"No, I did *not* have a free evening. I had a conference call, three supply contracts to approve and an accounting meeting that lasted past ten."

"But you're free now." He opened up the case.

She stared pointedly down at her robe. "Do I look free?"

He fought a grin. "You look…"

"Forget it."

"I was going to say cute."

"You were going to say awful."

His brow furrowed for a split second. "Why do you always—"

"What do you want, Alex?"

He shook his head, then he lifted an envelope from his briefcase. "I want to swap financial statements."

"Call me in the morning." She wanted to sleep. Nothing more, nothing less.

"I'm booked up all day."

"Well, I'm booked up all night."

He stilled. His glance shot to her bedroom door. "You have company?"

It took a moment for his meaning to set in. Of all the nerve. "*No*, I do not *have company*."

"I thought maybe you were having a final fling."

"I'm not a final fling kind of girl."

He checked her out one more time. "Really?"

"And if I was, would I dress like this?"

"I told you, you look cute."

She groaned in frustration.

He abandoned his briefcase and moved toward her. "Seriously, Emma. I don't know where all this insecurity comes from."

She had no idea how to respond to that. Zero.

His voice went soft. "You're a beautiful woman."

"Stop it," she rasped. He was obviously practicing his lines, spinning his lies, trying to put her off balance for his own reasons.

He came to a halt directly in front of her, the intensity of his perusal causing waves of reaction through her body. "Don't sell yourself short, Emma."

She tried to breathe normally, tried to squelch the unmistakable creep of desire working its way along her limbs. "You have… surprising taste."

His mouth curved into a slow grin.

It was a smooth mouth, a shapely mouth, a very sexy mouth, set under a luminous laserlike gaze that surrounded a woman and made her feel like the only person on the planet. Emma felt herself being dragged under his spell.

"You think I prefer silk and satin?" he asked softly.

"I think you'd prefer black lace and heels." As soon as she spoke, she regretted the impulse.

His nostrils flared ever so slightly. *"Really?"* And his eyes telegraphed his thoughts.

"Not on *me.*"

He glanced at her cleavage. "Why not?"

This was getting crazy. "Alex."

He nodded to her bedroom door. "You got something back there I might like?"

God help her, she did. A little teddy and matching panties that Katie had bought her on her birthday.

Not that Alex would ever see them.

A trace of laughter rumbled deep in his chest. "Still waters run deep?"

"I have nothing," she lied.

He reached up and smoothed a stray lock of her hair. "Sure you do. Go ahead, Emma. Let me in on your deep, dark secret."

She blinked into the polished obsidian of his eyes, steeling herself against his pull, promising herself she wouldn't let him take control of their relationship. She needed to stay strong. She needed to stay focused. She had something he wanted, and the transfer was going to be on *her* terms.

But then his palm paused on her temple, distracting her thoughts. His fingertips brushed her hair, and every reluctant nerve in her body zeroed in on his point of contact, zinging hormonal messages that flushed her skin and softened her lips, and pushed her body in toward him.

His hand slipped down to her neck, cupping her hairline, pulling her slowly, inexorably toward him. His head tipped to one side, and she followed his lead, accommodating his advance, waiting, wondering, coming up on her toes in anticipation.

Then he stopped. She felt his hesitation as if it were her own. *Yes,* her primal brain screamed. *No,* her rational mind answered.

His breath puffed against her skin. "My own deep, dark secret is…" He paused. "That I…" Another pause. "Want…" Then he sighed. "Your financial statements."

The words were a dose of cold water.

And she was glad.

Truly.

Kissing Alex would have been a supremely stupid move. Not that she wouldn't be forced to kiss him at some point during this escapade. But it didn't have to be in her apartment, while they were alone, while she was half-naked.

What was she *thinking?*

She pulled determinedly away. "Okay. But then you do have to go."

He gave her a sharp nod of agreement, blinking away a funny glow that simmered deep in his quick-silver eyes.

She wasn't going to explore that glow. She wasn't even going to think about that glow. This was business.

All *business,* she told herself as she crossed to her computer. She clicked a link to the financial server and brought up the last quarter rollups, hitting the print button.

Alex watched in silence as the printer whirred to life and rapidly spit out twenty pages.

She scooped them from the tray and briskly handed them over.

"Thank you," he said, as he reached for the doorknob.

"You're welcome," she replied, calculating the seconds until he'd be gone.

But then he paused, and his flinty eyes narrowed. His lips parted. "Emma—"

"Good night," she prompted with finality.

He sucked a breath between his teeth, but he didn't persist. Instead, he gave a brief nod of resignation. "Good night."

And then he was gone. She twisted the door lock behind him, her fingers clamping hard on the metal bolt. Okay *that*—whatever it was—could *not* happen again.

She'd made a deal with Alex. It was no different than her staffing the front desk in Hawaii or taking a stint as a cocktail waitress in Whistler. Her father had always been proud of Emma's ability to roll up her sleeves and pitch in.

In this case, maybe she was rolling up her lips. But it was the same thing. She'd kiss Alex eventually, but it would be a business kiss. It would be for show, and it sure wouldn't happen while they were alone and she was half naked and lusting after his body.

She shivered, stepping back from the door, telling herself she was doing exactly what her father would have done. She was making the best of a bad situation.

When her mother died, and he was left with two bereft little girls, he'd picked himself up and dusted himself off. He'd learned to braid their hair, wallpaper their rooms and bake chocolate chip oatmeal monster cookies. When their Montreal hotel burned to the ground, he'd made the best of that, too. With fearless, unflagging optimism, he'd buried his remorse, swept up the ashes and rallied the troops.

Well, Emma could be fearless. And she could bury whatever knee-jerk hormones were messing with her reaction to Alex. She'd make her father proud or die trying.

Emma was on guard Saturday night.

When they pulled into Tavern on the Green, she waited until Alex stepped out of the limo before she moved across the back seat. Mindful of the reporters waiting on the other side of the red rope line, she smoothed her champagne cocktail dress, and readied herself for a graceful exit.

Next to the open door, Alex turned to face her.

He gallantly offered his hand, and she bit back a protest. She didn't want to touch him at all, definitely not first thing. But there was no way to refuse the invitation.

Surrounded by the tiny white tree lights and the glowing lanterns of the portcullis, she took a breath and reached out. As soon as their fingertips made contact, a warm glow whooshed up her arm. She smiled bravely as cameras flashed in all directions.

Her gaze caught on Alex's soft, gray eyes. But she quickly blinked her attention away as he played out his role for the cameras. She tried to appear adoring without actually looking at his face—bad enough he was holding her hand. Bad enough she was imagining some cosmic connection between them as they strode the gauntlet of reporters firing questions.

Then Alex wrapped an arm around her waist and brought her to a halt for the photographers. They were pressed together, from knee to shoulder, and she could feel every single breath he took.

"Act like you adore me," he muttered under his breath.

"I'm trying," she returned, holding a smile,

cursing her traitorous body that was cataloguing every nuance of Alex.

"Try harder." He gave the photographers a final wave, then propelled her toward the entrance.

Emma resisted the pressure of his hand on the small of her back. "Katie and David were right behind us."

"They can catch up."

"But—"

"Until you become a better actress, we're not standing around for the paparazzi."

"I'm smiling, already."

"That's a grimace."

"That's because I'm in pain."

His arm immediately slacked off. "I'm hurting you?"

"Mental anguish." And that wasn't a lie.

"Give me a break." He resumed the pressure on the small of her back as a balding man in a finely cut suit stepped forward to greet them.

"Mr. Garrison," said the man with obvious enthusiasm. "So very good of you to join us."

"Good evening, Maxim," said Alex, reaching out to shake hands. "May I present my um, girl-friend, Emma McKinley."

His voice softened ever so slightly over her name. Emma's heart tripped for a split second, while Maxim did a double take.

"Maxim is the chairman of Teddybear Trust," Alex explained.

The burly man smiled broadly as he reached for Emma's hand. "And you're the president of McKinley Inns. We haven't met. But I've heard a good deal about you, Ms. McKinley."

"Please, call me Emma." Her smile was genuine now. "I have the utmost respect for the Teddybear Trust."

The foundation had built a new children's wing at St. Xavier's last year, and they'd funded countless pediatric cancer research projects.

"This way," said Maxim, gesturing through the cut glass doorway to the Tavern on the Green foyer. "Drinks are in the Terrace Room. And might I suggest the Pavilion as a starting point for casino games?"

"Blackjack?" asked Alex, tossing Maxim a wry grin.

Maxim grinned back. "Last year was unfortunate for you." Then he winked at Emma. "But I know you'll bring him good luck tonight."

"I'll try my best," she promised Maxim, thinking that karmic forces might not be so quick to reward them for lying to the entire city.

Then Alex recaptured her hand and nodded to the doorman as he placed a quick kiss on her knuckles. Emma struggled to keep her head clear as they crossed into the richly decorated entry. The lobby was festooned with fine crystal and stained glass, while magnificent chandeliers refracted light as they started their way through the winding hallways.

She caught their reflection in a beveled mirror, shivering at the image of Alex, straight and tall, his strong hand resting on the small of her back, only a hair below the plunging V of her sparkling dress.

"Would you care for a drink?" His deep voice rumbled through her.

"A Chablis," she replied, then cleared her throat against the sultry sound. They were playacting here. He was pretending to be her date for the benefit of the reporters and the other patrons. And she was pretending to like him for exactly the same end.

She dragged her gaze away from the mirror

and vowed to ignore every facet of his sex appeal. She needed to get a grip here.

He pointed to a doorway. "Through there, then."

They entered the Crystal Pavilion, catching the obviously curious glances of other guests.

Did they recognize Alex? Did they recognize her? She craned her neck, looking behind her for her sister's reassuring face. "We've lost Katie and David."

"We don't need a chaperone."

"But—"

"Tonight's about you and me." He smiled, nodded and waved a greeting to someone across the room.

They stopped next to the bar, and Alex rested a forearm on the polished top, giving the waiter their order before turning his attention to Emma. "You should try to relax and enjoy yourself."

Emma couldn't imagine relaxing under these circumstances. She couldn't imagine relaxing around Alex at all.

"In a few minutes you get to start spending my money," he said.

"I've never gambled in my life." She didn't mean it to sound snippy, but it came out that way.

"Somehow that doesn't surprise me." He snagged a handful of nuts from a crystal bowl on the bar and tossed them in his mouth.

"What's that supposed to mean?"

"It means you're way too conservative."

The waiter set the drinks down on Teddybear Trust coasters.

"I am not," Emma insisted.

Alex stuffed a bill in the tip snifter and nodded his thanks to the man. "Are too," he chuckled low to Emma as they walked away.

She huffed out a breath.

"You can prove me wrong, you know." He handed her the glass of Chablis, gently steering her back to the hallway. "Just belly on up to the blackjack table and make sure everyone knows I'm bankrolling you."

She took a sip of the crisp wine and let the alcohol ease into her system. "Is that what the modern urban male does for the woman he loves?"

"Since it's no longer practical to slay you a mastodon. Yeah. That's what we do."

She hid an unexpected grin behind another sip of the wine. "What if I want the mastodon instead?"

"Are you going high maintenance on me?"

"Apparently."

He pointed to another entryway. "Through here to the tables."

"Truthfully, I don't know how to play blackjack."

He shrugged. "It's easy."

Beyond the glass wall, lighted gardens spread out before them, lanterns swaying in the breeze as the well-dressed guests mingled from the restaurant to the patio and back again. The dealers, dressed in black jackets and bow ties, chatted with the guests as they doled out the cards.

Alex steered her toward a green felt table with high chairs and small white squares printed on the fabric.

"Hop up," he whispered against her ear, and she tried not to react to his nearness.

But then his arm casually brushed her bare back, raising goose bumps and sending pulses of energy to very inappropriate spots on her body.

"There you are." Katie's voice interrupted the moment. "This is fabulous!"

"Fabulous," Emma echoed, grateful for the buffer.

Katie hopped up next to Emma. There were already two men at the opposite end, of the table facing the dealer. That left one empty seat in the middle.

David stood behind Katie's chair, and Emma gave him a smile.

"Buy me some chips," Katie told him.

In her peripheral vision, Emma saw Alex place some bills on the table in front of the dealer.

"I thought we were going to the roulette wheel," David said to Katie.

Katie patted the tabletop. "I want to play blackjack."

The dealer slid four stacks of purple chips in front of Emma. She half turned to Alex. "What do I do now?" she whispered.

She could almost feel his smile. She inhaled his scent, and the fabric of his suit gently touched her bare back.

"Make a bet," he whispered back. "Put it in the white square."

The man at the far end bet two green chips, and the other bet a black one.

"What are the colors?" she asked Alex.

"Don't worry about it."

The dealer placed stacks of black chips in front of Katie.

Emma pushed two purple ones into the square in front of her, and the dealer gave them each a face-up card.

She glanced at everyone's cards, wondering if the man had made a mistake. She leaned back to talk to Alex. "They can see—"

"It's okay. You're only playing the dealer."

"Well, the dealer can see what I've got," she hissed. How was that fair?

"Trust me."

Emma tipped her head to look into his eyes. Trust him? Was he kidding? He'd made it clear last night—somewhere between gross revenue and capital depreciation—that he was looking out for his own interests. In fact, he'd strongly advised her to do the same.

Of course, in this case, it was his money. Who cared if she lost?

"Emma?"

"Hmmm?"

He nodded at the table. "Look at your hand."

She glanced down. A queen and an ace.

"You won," he said as the dealer pushed a couple of chips into her square.

"Hit me," said Katie next to her.

Even though it was just luck, a warm glow of pride grew in Emma's chest. She'd won. Her very first time gambling, and she'd won. Whatever happened from here on in, at least she had that.

"Bust," sighed Katie, while David shook his head.

The dealer cleared the cards.

"Bet more this time," said Alex.

Emma stacked another chip in her square.

"It's going to be a long night at this rate," Alex breathed.

"Why don't you do it then?"

He leaned in closer, his hand sliding up to her bare shoulder. "Because we want the world to see *me* spending a lot of money on *you*, remember?"

She turned so that her nose almost contacted his cheek. His spicy scent surrounded her, and his broad palm moved ever so slightly against her shoulder. It would be so easy to sink into this fantasy.

She reached for her wine. "How about if you bet my money instead?"

He chuckled. "Doesn't work that way. Now bet."

"You're such a chauvinist."

"Yeah, I am. Get used to it." He straightened, ending the conversation.

Fine. He wanted to bankroll her? Emma moved an entire stack of chips into the white square. *Take that, Alex Garrison.*

"That a girl," he said.

"Holy crap, Emma," said Katie.

Emma turned to her sister.

"That's ten thousand dollars."

"What?" Emma nearly swallowed her tongue.

The first card landed in front of her.

"Those are five-hundred-dollar chips," Katie pointed out.

Emma's stomach contracted. She quickly reached for the stack of chips, but Alex stopped her by putting his hand over hers.

"Too late," he warned.

She turned to stare at him, her eyes wide in horror. She couldn't bet ten thousand dollars on a hand of cards. That was nuts.

"Play the game," he calmly advised.

"Why didn't you *tell* me?"

"Tell you what?"

"Alex."

"Play the game."

"No way." She started to rise, but her hand was trapped by his.

"You won," he said.

"What?"

He nodded to her cards. "You won again. You really should gamble more often."

Emma slowly looked down at her hand, a ten and an ace. She gave in to her wobbly knees and sat back down on the stool.

"Bust," said Katie.

David shifted behind her.

"How much did you lose?" Emma asked her sister. David didn't look too happy about this.

"Five hundred dollars."

Emma cringed. "Ouch."

Katie tossed two more chips in her square.

"I think we should move to roulette," David suggested.

"This is fun," said Katie. "We're having fun. Aren't we, Emma?"

"I'm having fun," said Alex, a definite edge of laughter to his voice.

David's nostrils flared as he drew in a deep breath.

The dealer passed out the cards.

"You know you just let fifteen thousand dollars ride?" asked Katie.

Emma's gaze flew to her chips. Good God. Why hadn't Alex stopped her?

After a long, tense minute, she won with a three-card nineteen. She immediately swiveled her chair sideways. "I can't take this anymore."

Alex trapped the chair with one knee to keep it from recoiling. "You're winning."

Their legs touched, and the warmth of his body seeped into her thigh. "I'm having a heart attack," she told him. And it was definitely on more than one front.

She started to climb off the high stool, and he quickly offered a hand to steady her. "You don't walk away from a hot streak."

"Watch me."

She shifted. Whoops. She hadn't counted on being all but trapped in his arms. A half step forward and she'd be pressed up against him. If she tipped her head, they could kiss. Or she could bury her face in his neck and flick out her tongue to see if he tasted as good as he smelled.

Of course she didn't. But the desire was strong. So was the image.

He watched her with those smoky eyes for a long moment. "Okay." He finally said. "Ever played craps?"

"No."

"Good." Then he gestured toward the hallway, putting an end to the intimate moment. "Craps tables are in the Chestnut Room."

She turned to Katie. "Are you coming?"

"Not for craps," said David.

Katie peered at her boyfriend's expression. "We'll catch up," she told them.

Emma nodded. Then she began walking with Alex. "Can we at least switch to ten-dollar chips?"

"No."

"I can't bet five hundred dollars at a time."

Alex might be comfortable with a high-rolling, high-stakes lifestyle. But she sure wasn't.

"You're already up several thousand," he said.

That was true. She felt a little better. She could lose all this, and he'd still be even.

"If you don't start losing soon," Alex continued. "The Teddybear Trust will be bankrupt."

Emma stopped, and her mouth formed a spontaneous O. She'd forgotten all about the Teddybear Trust. "I'm doing this all wrong, aren't I?"

Alex chuckled, his hand going to her back to get her going again. "I'll say."

She gave a sigh of frustration.

Then, unexpectedly, his lips brushed her temple. "You're delightful, you know that?"

Her chest contracted around the compliment.

But then Edwina and Fredrick Waddington materialized next to Alex, and she realized the compliment was part of the ruse. Everything about tonight was part of the ruse. Alex wasn't an easygoing, philanthropic businessman. He was only playing his part.

She forced out a smile as he performed the introductions. No more fantasy. No more intimacy. No more physical reactions. From this minute on, she was remembering it was a game.

Four

No matter how hard Emma tried, she couldn't seem to lose. A crowd had gathered around one of the craps tables, and every time she attempted to pass the dice, they'd erupt in a torrent of protest, shoving them back into her hands.

She took a deep breath.

Standing behind her, Alex rubbed her shoulders. "With a bet like that, you're either going to save the charity or buy us a new hotel."

She shook the dice up between her hands. "We don't need a new hotel. This is getting embarrassing. Don't you see Maxim glaring at me?"

"He's not glaring at you."

Emma glanced surreptitiously at her host and watched him run a finger under the collar of his shirt. It was bad enough that she was winning. But the entire crowd was winning along with her.

"How do I lose?" she whispered to Alex.

"Roll a seven."

"Okay." She blew on the dice.

Alex chuckled at her theatrics, and she dug her elbow into his ribs.

"A little support, please," she breathed.

"Come on, seven," he rumbled in return. "You do know you'll lose two hundred grand."

"It's not my money."

"Yeah. It's mine." Despite his protest, he sounded completely unconcerned.

It wasn't his money anyway. It was the Teddybear Trust's money. And she was going to put it back where it belonged or die trying.

She tossed the dice. They scattered along the green felt table, bouncing amongst bets that probably totaled a surgical wing, hitting the far wall of the table, then rolling to a stop. A six and a one.

Delight zipped through her.

She'd done it.

"Quit grinning," Alex warned as the crowd groaned.

Right. The other betters were disappointed. She quickly hid her smile against Alex's chest.

His strong arms went around her, and he made a show of stroking her back.

Okay. So much for not reacting to his latent sensuality. Every fiber of her body was revving up in reaction to his heat.

"Don't worry," he said, loud enough for everyone else to hear. "It's only money. And it's for a good cause."

The groans and grumbles around them gradually turned to good-natured jokes. One man pointed out the tax benefits of their loss, while another suggested they'd all be on Teddybear Trust's Christmas card list this year.

Alex didn't seem to be in a hurry to let her go. No wonder. He had a big audience here—a big audience that would soon start asking questions about their relationship.

Hugging was the smart thing to do. So for just a second, Emma stopped fighting. She relaxed into his strength and let the tension roll out of her body. Gambling was way too stress-ful, even when she was trying to lose.

Alex's palm smoothed her hair, while his lips touched the top of her head in a tender kiss. It felt way too good, and sirens went off in all corners of her brain.

She ignored them as long as she could. But finally she pulled back. Still, he kept one arm firmly around her waist. Although it went against her mental promise, she didn't try to disentangle herself.

Some of the players moved away from the table, and the stick man called for a new shooter.

Katie and David appeared from the crowd.

"How'd you do?" asked Katie.

"She lost all my money," said Alex with a playful squeeze.

"Well, it has gone to a good cause," Emma pointed out.

"You lost my entire thirty-thousand-dollar stake," said Alex.

She'd forgotten it was that much.

But one glance at his expression told her he didn't care. Certainly he didn't care. He wanted the whole world to know she was here on his dime.

That was the game. His *game,* she reminded herself, trying to ease out of his hold. "Take the tax deduction and quit complaining."

He resisted her pressure.

She tugged harder.

Alex just grinned at her.

"Ladies and gentlemen," Maxim's voice came over the sound system. "You're invited to take a break from the casino games and join us in the garden for a surprise, grand prize draw."

"The gardens are lovely," said Emma, pulling firmly out of Alex's grip and moving to safety beside her sister. "Let's go watch the draw."

"Thanks to the generosity of an anonymous donor," Maxim continued. "Our grand prize this year is a Mercedes-Benz convertible."

The crowd gave an appreciative *ahh.*

"Check the top right corner of your admission ticket for your lucky draw number."

Emma linked arms with Katie and they followed the flow of people moving toward the lighted greenery. She was trying to focus on the gardens, on Katie, on *anything* but Alex. Or, more to the point, on anything but her reaction to Alex.

"Is David okay?" she asked Katie, concentrating on how the oak trees sparkled with thousands of white lights and lines of lanterns glowed against colorful flower tubs and hanging baskets. The garden was absolutely breathtaking at night.

Katie shrugged her shoulders. "Why do you ask?"

Emma studied her sister's expression. "He seems quiet." David was normally joking and jovial. Kind of like how Alex was tonight.

Nope, wait. Not Alex. *Not* Alex.

"Maybe he thought I'd win," said Katie.

"How much did you lose?"

"A couple of thousand." Katie tossed her blond hair. "I really don't know what his problem is." Then she whistled low, pointing to the car. "Oh, baby. I can sure see myself cruising around the park in that."

"Not bad," Emma agreed, checking out the sleek lines of the silver convertible. The chrome shone, and the paint fairly glowed under the brilliance of the garden lights.

"Ladies and gentlemen," came Maxim's voice

as he stepped up onto the dais next to the spectacular car. "I have to say, Teddybear Trust donors are the most generous people in the country!"

A cheer went up from the crowd.

He bobbed his head in acknowledgement of the gesture.

Then, as the applause died down, he reached into a crystal bowl, stirring the slips of paper around with great drama. "And…the winner of this gorgeous, brand-new Mercedes-Benz convertible is…number seven-thirty-two!"

Alex ruffled Emma's hair from behind. "That's mine," he murmured in her ear. Then he leaned up and winked. "I'll be right back."

Emma stared at his retreating back. "He won?" she asked out loud.

Katie stared at her for a moment, her blue eyes going wide. "He won!" she cried.

"I see we have a winner," called Maxim as he spotted Alex moving through the crowd. Alex stepped up smartly onto the stage and handed Maxim his ticket.

"Mr. Alex Garrison," Maxim announced after a cursory glance. "Tonight's winner, and one of Teddybear Trust's most valued sponsors."

Alex made a show of sizing up the car. Then he stepped up to the microphone at the small podium. "Lady luck is definitely with me tonight," he announced with a broad grin. "And I'm hoping she'll stick around for a few more minutes."

He turned to Maxim. "Many, many thanks to Maxim and all of the dedicated volunteers at Teddybear Trust." He paused, gazing at the car for another moment. "Although I'd dearly love to take this baby out for a spin on the expressway, I'm afraid that won't be possible."

The crowd went silent.

"Because I'm donating it back to Teddybear," said Alex. "For their September auction."

Applause burst out as Maxim stepped forward and clasped Alex's hand with both of his.

Emma couldn't help the surge of pride that rose in her chest. Act or not, Alex had just donated serious money to a good charity.

He turned back to the microphone. "If you'll be patient with me for another minute. There's one more thing I want to say." He cleared his throat. "I was only half joking about lady luck. Truth is, I attribute tonight's luck to one very special lady." He stepped back for a beat.

"Emma," he continued, nodding in her direction.

It was a little overboard as courtship went. But, okay. She could go along. He'd earned this one. She smiled warmly up at him, trying to look love-struck.

He grinned back, his obsidian eyes sparkling under the tree lights. "Emma, will you do me the honor... Will you marry me?"

Emma froze. Her stomach plummeted to the patio.

A collective gasp went up from the crowd, followed quickly by a smattering of applause that grew and grew, while heads turned her way.

This was as bad as the JumboTron. No, it was worse than the JumboTron. At least at a baseball game, she'd have some anonymity. Half the people here tonight knew her, or had known her father.

Katie nudged her, and she realized Alex was staring at her expectantly.

While she tried to form a coherent thought, he reached into his pocket and pulled out a small velvet box. He'd planned this, the rat.

He was the anonymous car donor. The entire

evening of chivalry and philanthropy had been designed to back her into a corner.

"Emma, say something," Katie hissed.

"I can't," she whimpered under her breath.

"We made a deal with him," Katie reminded her.

Yes, they'd made a deal. But not for this. Not for such a ridiculous showy, sentimental display. Her reputation was at stake. And, besides, she'd specifically vetoed this very thing.

Katie gave her a slight shove toward the dais. "Get up there."

She wasn't going up there. She couldn't do it. Her feet had become concrete.

"Emma?" Alex singsonged in an overblown, adoring voice. The faker.

"Bankruptcy," whispered Katie in a warning tone.

Bankruptcy.

Emma forced one foot forward. Then she moved the other. Then she pasted a sickly-sweet smile on her face and made her way toward him.

The crowd's applause escalated, and people congratulated her all along the short route. She let her vision go soft, and the multitude of faces blur in front of her.

Up on the stage, Alex gallantly took her hand. "Will you marry me?" he repeated, popping open the velvet box.

She barely glanced at the ring. She just wanted to get this over with and get out of there. She hastily nodded her head. "Yes. Yes, I'll marry you." *And then I'm going to kill you.*

His grin said he was reading her mind again. It also said he'd won this round. He took the marquise solitaire out of the box and slipped it onto her finger.

Then, as the crowd roared its approval, he leaned down.

He wasn't…

He wouldn't…

He *would!*

She tried to step back, but his arms slid around her.

Under his breath, he commanded, "Kiss me." And she realized she had no choice.

Several hundred people were watching, and this was the crux of a multimillion dollar deal. She tipped her head and saw him smile.

She promised herself she'd make it quick. She'd pucker up, get it done and get the heck away from this sham. But then his lips touched hers, igniting twenty-four hours' worth of pent-up passion.

His mouth was warm and firm, and way too mobile for a perfunctory photo op. Fine smoky scotch had flavored his lips, the residual alcohol tingling her sensitive skin.

She told herself to end it, but his arms pulled her tight, and fireworks went off inside her head, counterpoint to the flashes of cameras in her peripheral vision. A primal hormone kicked in, and her eyes fluttered closed. Her body went limp, and she opened to him, giving him access, returning his parry, her body alight in raw desire.

Ever so slowly, his arms loosened. Then he drew back, finishing with a brief, tender peck on her ravaged lips. Then the cheers of the crowd penetrated her consciousness, as every photographer in the place finished a montage of their kiss.

A cold wash of reality hit Emma. Keeping a professional distance was going to be a lot more difficult than she'd imagined.

* * *

Alex couldn't believe how easy that had been. Maxim had been more than eager to participate in the Mercedes scam. Sure, it meant Teddybear got a sizable donation, but Alex had a feeling the man was more excited about the flamboyant engagement. Whatever.

Alex shrugged as his limo pulled away from the portcullis in front of the McKinley Fifth Avenue. He'd seen Emma to the penthouse elevator and now picked up the phone to dial Ryan's number. He guessed a lot of people had a romantic streak.

"Yo," said Ryan in a sleepy voice.

"The ring's on her finger," said Alex as the limo turned into traffic.

"It went well?"

"She said yes." That was the salient point. The kiss had seemed salient there for a few minutes, too. Surprisingly salient. But the kiss was fleeting, even if it was unexpectedly arousing. That diamond ring was money in the bank. "Boy Scout Garrison is now *Romantic Fool* Boy Scout Garrison." Gunter would be thrilled with the publicity, but Alex sure wasn't wild about the inherent celibacy.

"Better you than me, buddy," Ryan chuckled, knowing full well the engagement had clipped Alex's dating wings.

A soft murmur sounded in the background, cuing Alex's radar.

"You alone?" he asked.

"You kidding?"

Alex swore.

Ryan chuckled again. "Grit your teeth and think of the profit."

"I am thinking about the profit." But Alex was also thinking about Emma's kiss. For someone who prided herself on her solemn strength, her lips sure packed a punch. And she'd looked fantastic in that sparkling dress that showed off miles of creamy smooth skin.

He'd run his fingertips over it as often as he'd dared. Which turned out to be a mistake, since it was hard to think about the money when all he wanted was more of her body and more of her lips. And that wasn't about to happen in any meaningful way. Not now, not ever.

The woman with Ryan giggled, and Alex heaved a frustrated sigh.

"Buck up," Ryan advised.

"Right." Alex stabbed the end button and tossed the phone on the bench seat beside him. It was going to be a *very* long marriage.

Emma had had a very long Monday morning.

The following morning, she wiped away the sweat that had gathered near her hairline, tuning out the chatter of two women in a whirlpool tub near the spa's fern garden.

She should have known better than to get mixed up with Alex. When a deal was too good to be true, it meant it was *too good to be true.* Yeah, the man was bailing them out financially, but the personal price was much too high.

She hated the spotlight. And if this morning's flurry of activity was anything to go by, the spotlight was exactly where she'd be stuck for the next few months. Out of desperation, she'd left her office, skulked down the back staircase and dragged a lounger behind the curve of the marble wall here in the hotel spa in a bid for peace and privacy.

"Emma?" came Katie's voice from around a spreading palm.

"Back here," Emma reluctantly confirmed.

Katie appeared in high heels, a straight white skirt and a matching blazer. "What are you doing?"

Emma paused for a significant second. "What do you *think* I'm doing?"

"I don't know."

"Well, I'm hiding."

"From *what?*"

"Not from what, from who."

Katie stripped off her blazer. "Then who?"

"Philippe."

"Why? And aren't you going to ruin your laptop?"

"Because he's a caterer. And because he's an insane stalker. And yes, probably."

The two women in a nearby whirlpool laughed, and Katie took a couple of steps closer, lowering her voice. "You're being stalked by an insane caterer? Is there such thing as an insane caterer?"

"I think they're all insane," said Emma. "I'm being stalked by at least a dozen. Philippe is just the most persistent of the crowd."

"Can't security take care of them?"

Emma pressed the save button on her laptop

and turned her complete attention to Katie. "Oh, sure. Then all the reporters can have a field day on McKinley security staff roughing up skinny men in berets."

Katie glanced behind her. "We have reporters, too?"

Emma sighed and pushed back her damp hair. "Yes. We have reporters. In the lobby, out front, on the mezzanine floor."

"Nobody bothered me."

"That's because Alex Garrison didn't make a spectacle of you last night."

Katie took a seat on the far end of the lounger, curling one leg beneath her as her face lit up with the memory. "You have to admit, if that had been real, it would have been incredibly romantic."

Emma didn't have to admit any such thing. It was grandiose and tacky. She'd never, not in a million years, marry a man who thought proposing in public was romantic.

She snapped the laptop closed. "It wasn't real."

Katie sighed. "I know that."

"So quit getting all starry-eyed on me. Alex was *acting*." A small difference, maybe. But a rather important one.

Katie toyed with a lock of her hair. "He's a good actor."

"He probably had his marketing staff coach him."

Katie laughed at that.

"Mademoiselle McKinley?" came a nasal male voice.

A sudden shift in Emma's blood pressure left her feeling light-headed. She stared at Katie. "You were *followed?*"

"I'm not exactly double-o-seven," Katie protested.

"Aarrgghh."

"Mademoiselle McKinley?" Philippe Gagnon repeated. Then he appeared around the corner of the marble wall. "Ah, *there* you are."

Katie nearly choked on a laugh as the brisk, wiry sixty-something man stepped in front of them and clasped his palms together over his chest.

"There is so much we must do," he began.

He sure had that right. And on the top of Emma's list was a clandestine trip to the Bahamas. She'd find a small secluded beachfront hut with no phone, no radio, and *no* caterers.

Katie, on the other hand, seemed completely unperturbed by Philippe's interruption. She stood and held out her hand to him. "I'm Katie McKinley, sister of the bride."

"*Enchanté,* mademoiselle." He gallantly raised her hand to his lips and kissed her knuckles. "I am Philippe Gagnon. Sous chef, trained at the Sorbonne and apprenticed under John-Pierre Laconte. I have cooked for princes and presidents."

Katie turned to Emma, her grin growing wide. "Did you hear that, Emma? He's cooked for princes and presidents."

"Shoot me now," Emma muttered as a trickle of sweat made its way between her breasts.

Philippe shook an admonishing finger. "No, no. None of that from the bride. I am here now, and I will take care of everything."

Emma sat up straight. "Oh, no you—"

"*Emma.*" Katie shot her eyes a look of warning.

But Emma wasn't getting dragged into this circus. "I am not—"

"This is a most stressful time for you, mademoiselle." Philippe fluttered a hand toward the exit. "Those bohemian food hacks in the lobby. I will have them gone. Poof."

Then he held up his palms. "No, no. No need to thank me. After that, I will talk to the reporters. Give them a tidbit or two, non? Satisfy them for a short while."

Emma stared into the man's pale blue eyes, seeing an unexpected shrewdness in their depths. It took her less than a minute to revise her opinion of him. "You can get all those people out of my lobby?"

"But, of course," he said. "You must stay calm. I must keep you calm."

If by keeping her calm, Philippe meant protecting her privacy? He was hired.

Mrs. Nash punctuated her presence on the pool deck by clacking a pitcher of orange juice down on the table next to Alex's lounger.

He glanced up from the executive summary of the McKinley strategic plan.

He didn't know what he'd done to annoy Mrs. Nash, but it was obvious by the set of her lips that something was up. He tried to gauge her expression, but the sun was bright, and his eyes were grainy from lack of sleep.

He decided to go for the direct approach. "Something wrong?"

"What could be wrong?" Then her lips returned to the prune position. "Though I see you're getting married."

"I am," he confirmed, wondering if that was really the problem. Surely she wasn't offended because he hadn't told her personally. Sunday was her day off.

She peered at him over the half glasses that were secured around her neck by a sparkling gold chain.

He was clearly supposed to be catching onto something here. But he really didn't have time for games. Another ten minutes of cramming for the showdown with old man Murdoch from DreamLodge, and he was diving into the pool to wake himself up. He would barely get in thirty lengths and a shower if he wanted to be at the DreamLodge offices before eight.

And he definitely wanted to be there before the start of business. He wasn't taking any chances that Murdoch would get to Emma before Alex got to him.

Mrs. Nash finally relented. "To a woman I've never met?"

Alex gave his head a brief shake. "You met her last week."

Mrs. Nash drew in an expressive breath. "No. She was at the estate last week. We were never introduced."

Okay. That was an oversight. Alex could see that now, and he would definitely introduce them as soon as possible. "I'll—"

"And I see she's recently come into some property…"

And what, exactly, did Mrs. Nash mean by that? And what was that funny tilt to her chin?

Her tone dropped to interrogation timbre and the pace of her words slowed. "*Hotel* property."

"Yes." Alex measured his response. He was way too tired to justify his personal life.

At his admission, her voice turned snappy again. "You ought to be ashamed of yourself, young man."

Young man? "What happened to *Mr.* Garrison?"

"Sweeping that innocent girl off her feet."

Alex sat forward. "Wait a minute—"

"Did you send her the usual hothouse bouquet? Take her to Tradori's? Book your suite at the Manhattan?"

"Whoa." How did Mrs. Nash know about his suite at the Manhattan? "I've been completely up front with Emma."

"Ha. The poor woman didn't have a ghost of a chance. Her father only recently passing."

Now that just plain wasn't fair. Alex rose to his feet. "She had every chance."

Mrs. Nash shook her head. "Alex, I love you dearly. You are like a son to me."

"I didn't do anything wrong."

"I know your weaknesses."

"I know my weaknesses, too." And they certainly didn't include lying to women in order to steal their property.

They might involve misleading a competitor to cinch a business deal, or lying to the world at large in order to merge two hotel chains. But those were completely separate issues. And defensible ones.

Not that he had to explain himself.

Of course he didn't have to explain himself.

Unfortunately, something in her expression triggered a psychological remnant of his childhood. And he couldn't seem to bring himself to disappoint her.

He made a split-second decision to bring her into the circle. "Emma knows why I'm marrying her."

Mrs. Nash's expression changed. "She knows it's for her hotels?"

He nodded. "I offered her a financial bailout, and she took it. Now, if you'll excuse me, I have a meeting."

He stripped off his shirt, stepped out of his sandals to head across the deck.

Mrs. Nash followed on his heels. "A marriage of convenience, Mr. Garrison?"

"Yes, Mrs. Nash. A marriage of convenience." It wasn't like he was breaking the law.

"Well, we both know where that leads."

"To profitability and an increase in our capital asset base?"

"To misery and a cold, lonely death."

A stillness took over Alex's body. He hooked his toes over the edge and gazed into the still, clear water. "I am not my father."

"You are more like him than you care to admit."

"I'm nothing like him."

She clicked her teeth, and he could feel her shaking her head.

"I know what I'm doing, Mrs. Nash."

"Due respect, Mr. Garrison. You haven't a bloody clue."

Yeah. That was respectful all right. Alex tamped down the urge to engage in the debate. He was out of patience, and he was out of time. He drew a strangled breath, tensed his calf muscles and dove into the pool.

Five

It was three minutes past eight by the time Alex found a parking spot and strode up the wide staircase into the DreamLodge headquarters lobby. The airy, open room was impressive—quiet, understated and classy. But then Clive Murdoch hadn't built his empire on stupidity and poor taste. He was Alex's number one competitor for good reason. The man wasn't to be taken lightly.

Briefcase in hand, power suit freshly pressed, and his hair trimmed right to his collar, Alex scanned the floor directory next to a bank of elevators. The executive suite was on number thirty-eight.

He pressed a button and one of the doors immediately slid open.

The ride up was direct and smooth. And on the top floor, he emerged and introduced himself to the receptionist, hoping name recognition would get him in to see Clive Murdoch without an appointment.

"I'll see if he's free, Mr. Garrison." The young woman smiled behind a discreet headset and punched a number on her phone.

"Alex?" The sound of another woman's voice sent a ripple of warning up his spine.

He quickly blinked the surprise from his expression and turned to face Emma. Then he took a few steps forward to put some distance between them and the receptionist. "Emma," he crooned. "Right on time, I see."

"What are you—"

"I was worried you'd be late, sweetheart." He gave her a kiss on the forehead, while his mind scrambled for a contingency plan.

"What are you doing here?" she asked.

"What are *you* doing here?" he returned. "And why aren't you wearing your ring?" A good offense? It might work. He sure hadn't come up with any better ideas in the past fifteen seconds.

"I have an appointment," she said.

"So I heard," he bluffed.

"Heard from who?"

He quickly grabbed an answer for that one. "The hotel business is a tight-knit community."

She frowned. "It is not."

"Yes, it is." He frowned back at her, pretending he had a right to be annoyed. "I can't believe you'd book a meeting with Murdoch without me."

And, quite frankly, he couldn't believe she'd agree to meet Murdoch on his own turf for a negotiation. Didn't she understand the home court advantage?

"It's still my company," she said.

"And I'm a player in it. Where's your ring?"

She curled her left hand and tucked it behind her. "We haven't signed a thing."

They'd talk about the ring later. He had a lot to say about the damn ring. "You said yes in front of five hundred people."

Her complexion darkened a shade. "And we are *definitely* talking about that one later."

He should hate it when she used that tone of voice. But he didn't. It energized him instead of annoying him. It made him look forward to later.

"Fine," he said, keeping his tone deliberately flat. "But for now we have a meeting."

"*I* have a meeting."

He gave her a cold smile. "Sweetheart, your last solo business meeting was yesterday."

"Why, you—"

He cut her off with a quick kiss on her taut, tender lips. Then he drew back and dared her with his eyes, all the while raising his voice so the receptionist would hear. "Don't worry about it. We can pick up the ring after lunch."

"I'm going to kill you," she muttered under her breath.

"Later," he whispered. "After you give me hell for proposing to you." Then he took her hand and turned to the friendly receptionist. "Is Mr. Murdoch ready to see us?"

Emma couldn't believe Alex had crashed her business meeting. How had he found her? How had he even known to look for her? And didn't he have his own business to run on a Monday morning?

She felt like a fool traipsing into Clive Murdoch's office half a step behind him. She looked like a fool, too, if Clive's expression was anything to go by. He'd called last week to say he'd been working on a deal with her father. He wondered if she'd be taking over from here on in.

She'd said, "absolutely." She'd said she was at the helm, making decisions, running the company. And here Alex had cut her off at the knees.

"Clive," Alex greeted brusquely, sticking out his hand.

"Alex." Clive nodded, offering a guarded handshake.

He looked to Emma. "Ms. McKinley?"

"Soon to be Mrs. Garrison," said Alex, a definite edge of aggression in his tone.

Emma shot him a glare. What did he think he was doing?

"Good news travels fast," said Clive.

Alex pulled out a chair at the round meeting table, gesturing for Emma to sit in it.

She thought about rebuffing his offer, but his expression wasn't one to mess with. So she took the chair. She'd set him straight on business protocol later.

"Yet," said Alex, still standing, that same thread of steel in his tone. "You made an appointment with my fiancée anyway."

"Alex," Emma interrupted.

"I made the appointment last week," said Clive. His shoulders were tense, his voice hard-edged.

"Things have changed since last week," said Alex.

"Mr. Murdoch," said Emma, trying to calm things down.

"Call me Clive," said Clive.

"Don't," said Alex.

Emma stared at him in total shock. "Will you *stop* this?" Then she looked at Clive. "We're here to listen."

Alex's hands closed over the back of one of the chairs. "We're here to make a point."

She glared at Alex. "You don't even know—"

"McKinley assets are not for sale. Not now. Not ever. None of them."

For sale? Clive hadn't said anything about a sale.

"You haven't even heard my offer," Clive stated, the word *sale* obviously no surprise to him.

Emma stilled. How had Alex known they were talking about a sale? She hadn't even known they were talking about a sale.

"We don't need to hear your offer," said Alex. Then he reached out a hand to Emma. "In fact, we don't need to be here at all."

Emma glanced back and forth between the two men as they stared each other down. What had she missed? What did Clive want to buy? Why wouldn't Alex consider it?

"Can somebody please—"

"I'm your contact," Alex informed Clive, tossing a business card on the table. "You think you have any more business with McKinley, you call *me*."

Clive didn't touch the card. "You walk out that door, the offer's closed."

Alex shrugged, and it occurred to Emma he might be negotiating. Was this how it was normally done? Did he expect Clive to follow them to the lobby and up the ante?

Clive smirked. "The offer was *way* above market."

"It was chump change, and we both know it."

Wow. Emma could never have been that gutsy. She did wish she knew what they were talking about, but it seemed to make the most sense to play along.

She took Alex's hand, and they left the office.

"What now?" she asked as they waited for the elevator.

Alex glanced down at her. "Now, there's someone I want you to meet."

She glanced over her shoulder. "So, will he follow us?"

Alex looked behind them. "I doubt it."

"But…"

"But what?"

The elevator door slid open.

"I thought he'd follow us out and up the offer."

Alex gestured for her to precede him. "He didn't make an offer."

"But he was going to."

Alex trapped the elevator door to keep it from closing. "Yes, he was going to."

The truth dawned on Emma. "We really walked away without even hearing what it was?" What kind of a way was that to conduct business?

"Of course we walked away. Get on."

"But maybe it was—"

Alex leaned in, lowering his voice. "Stop talking and get in the elevator."

Emma hesitated. Then her glance slid over to the receptionist. Right. This argument was unseemly. But what on earth was Alex thinking?

She lifted her chin and marched inside, gritting her teeth until the door closed. "Maybe it was good," she shouted. "Maybe it was *fantastic.*"

Alex gave a dry chuckle. "Which do you think is more likely, Emma? That Clive Murdoch got rich by benevolently paying more than market price for hotels, or that Clive Murdoch is a shrewd old man looking to take advantage of your inexperience."

She glared at Alex. "Guess we'll have to tell him to get in line for that one, won't we?"

A muscle near his temple ticked for a moment. "I'm not old. And I'm not taking advantage of you, Emma. I'm saving you from bankruptcy."

"Benevolently, I'm sure," she returned with syrupy sweetness. "And with no thought whatsoever for your own welfare."

"You knew the score from minute one."

The elevator pinged and the door glided open.

"How do I know you're not taking advantage of my inexperience?" she pressed. "And, by the way, that was insulting. I've been in the hotel business my entire life. I've done everything from tend bar to renovate a ski resort."

"That's your credential? Tending bar?"

"Most recently, I was the vice president of North American operations. I'm not some naive newbie."

"Yeah?" he challenged as they started across the lobby. "Then why did you agree to meet Murdoch in his office?"

Emma didn't get the point of the question. "Because it was Mr. Murdoch I was meeting with."

Alex pushed open the double glass doors. The temperature went up twenty degrees while car horns and tire screeches replaced the echoing quiet of the lobby. "You should have had him come to you."

"What difference would that make?"

They dodged other pedestrians as they made their way down the stairs.

"Tactical advantage." Alex's lips quirked in a grin. "Newbie mistake. Good thing I was there to rescue you."

"*You* didn't even let him make the offer."

"The offer sucked, Emma. I brought a car. Just across the street."

"You don't know that."

"No—I'm pretty sure I brought a car. That blue Lexus over there, under the red sign."

"You don't know the offer sucked."

Alex stopped at the bottom of the stairs and turned to face her. "I knew about your meeting. I knew he wanted to buy. I knew how to shut him down. Don't you think there's maybe a slim possibility that I know the market value of a hotel?"

"Not half high on yourself, are you?" As soon as the sarcastic words were out, Emma regretted them.

Alex had made a fair point.

She'd been out to prove herself on this deal with Murdoch. She'd even gone so far as to secretly hope that whatever he had in mind would save McKinley Inns, so that she wouldn't have to give half of the company to Alex, and she could avoid going through with this farce of a wedding.

But Murdoch hadn't wanted to make a business deal beneficial to McKinley. He'd simply wanted to make a purchase. He'd been looking for a bargain.

Not that she'd ever admit any of it to Alex. He had enough of an advantage over her already.

"Like I said before," Alex interrupted her thoughts. "There's somebody I want you to meet."

"Your lawyer?" Now that the engagement was out of the way, the prenup was next on the list.

"No. Not my lawyer. My housekeeper."

For a man with a reputation as a cold-blooded hard case, Alex sure had a soft spot for his housekeeper. Oh, he tried to hide it. But it was there in the inflection of his voice as they came down his long driveway in Oyster Bay.

"She can be irritable at times, and she's as judgmental as anyone I've ever met. But she's been with the family since before I was born, so I try to humor her."

"Because she scares the life out of you," Emma guessed.

Alex hesitated just a shade too long. "Don't be ridiculous."

They drove beneath spreading oaks and past fine-trimmed lawns. The last time Emma had come to the Garrison estate, she'd been focused on the upcoming conversation with Alex. This time she paid more attention to the landscaping, doing a double take as they passed a magnificent rose garden.

"What did you tell her about me?" Emma asked as she craned her neck to watch the stunning blooms. *Wow.* The Vanderbilts' gardener had nothing on the Garrisons'.

"That I was marrying you for your hotels," he said.

"You did not."

"Actually, I told her I was helping you out of a financial jam. She guessed the part about the hotels."

That surprised Emma. "Well, at least I don't have to lie to her."

"You don't have to lie to anyone else either."

Okay, now that was about the most ridiculous thing Emma had ever heard. "Yeah, I have to lie."

"We tell them we're getting married," he explained. "We tell them we couldn't be happier—which, when you consider the money, has got to be true. And we tell them we're co-managing McKinley Inns. All perfectly valid."

"And what do we do when they ask about our feelings? You planning to pull a Prince Charles?"

He glanced her way, raising an eyebrow. "A Prince Charles?"

"When Prince Charles was asked if he loved Diana, he said 'whatever love is.'"

Alex chuckled.

"Hey, you pull a Prince Charles on me, and I'll pull a Mrs. Nash on you."

"What's a Mrs. Nash?"

"I don't know, but she does something that intimidates you, and I'm going to find out what it is."

"You're crazy."

"Like a fox." Emma glanced back out the windshield to see the three-story white building rising up in front of them. "I swear your house is bigger than some of my hotels."

"That's why I bought an apartment in Manhattan."

"You kept getting lost?"

Alex laughed.

The building grew closer and seemed to get

taller. White stone pillars gleamed in the morning sun. Dozens of dormered windows delineated the three, no, *four* stories, while a fountain dominated the circular drive's center garden.

"You spin me around three times in there, I swear you'll never have to see me again."

"Good tip," said Alex as he brought the car to a smooth halt in front of the polished staircase.

She pulled a face, but he just laughed at her.

They exited the car and started climbing the wide steps.

"We have to talk about this," said Emma, trying not to feel outdone by Alex's status and old money.

"About my house?"

"About everything. How this marriage thing is going to work. How much time we'll have to spend together. How we'll coordinate our schedules."

Alex reached for the handle on the massive front door. "We can coordinate schedules over breakfast."

She supposed they could schedule a regular morning call. "What time do you get up?"

"Around six."

Emma nodded. "I usually eat about seven. We could talk on the phone over coffee."

"The phone?"

"You'd rather e-mail?"

"I'd rather eat at the same table. Dining room, breakfast nook, kitchen, pool deck, I don't care—"

"What are you talking about?"

He reached for the ornate knob on the huge double doors. "Breakfast. Pay attention, Emma. We're talking about breakfast."

"*Where?*"

"Here, of course."

Emma stopped dead. "Here?"

"Can you think of a better place?"

"My penthouse."

He smirked as he pushed open the door. "You want to share your bedroom with me?"

"We don't have to live together."

"Sure we do. We'll be married."

In name only. And even if they did spend time in the same residence, it couldn't be here.

Emma walked tentatively into the cavernous rotunda foyer, gazing upward. It definitely couldn't be here. "Regular people don't live like this," she said. "It's practically a palace."

"That's because great-great-great Grandpa Hamilton was British royalty. The second son of an earl."

Emma gazed at the row of portraits sweeping off down the main hallway. "Why does that not surprise me?"

"The Earl of Kessex," said Alex. "It's a small holding just south of Scotland. However, his older brother inherited the property and the title. So Hamilton became an admiral in the British navy. I guess he always wanted the trappings because he bought the original eight hundred acres and built this place."

Emma made her way slowly down the hallway, peering at the old portraits of nobility.

"This guy," said Alex, pointing to a distinguished man in a dress navy uniform, gold tassels on his shoulders, medals adorning his chest, with a saber clutched in his left hand. He looked proud, serious, intense. In fact, take away the hat, the moustache and about twenty-five years, and he looked surprisingly like Alex.

Emma stepped back and glanced from one to the other.

"Yeah, yeah," said Alex. "I know."

"It explains a lot," said Emma. "It's genetics that make you so intent on expanding the family empire."

"Oh, I *like* her," came a woman's voice. She had a British accent, and her staunch declaration was quickly followed by the tapping of her heels on the hardwood floor.

Embarrassed, Emma pulled away from Alex.

The woman was taller than Emma, maybe five feet ten in her sensible shoes. Her hair was dyed sandy blond and cut fashionably short so that it feathered around her narrow face. She had on a straight skirt, a high collar and minimal makeup, and a pair of reading glasses dangled from a gold chain around her neck.

"You don't deserve her," the woman said to Alex.

"Mrs. Nash. May I present Emma McKinley, my fiancée."

It was the fist time Alex had used the title, and it made Emma's stomach clamp with guilt.

"You're quite certain you want to do this?"

Mrs. Nash asked Emma, carefully searching her expression.

"Quite certain," said Emma. And she was. There were a million reasons against marrying Alex. But the one reason in favor of marrying him was pretty compelling.

"Well, let's get a look at you, then." Mrs. Nash glanced her up and down with a critical eye.

"*Mrs. Nash,*" Alex protested.

"Amelia's," she pronounced.

Emma looked to Alex.

"Emma can pick her own wedding dress," said Alex.

Her wedding dress? So far Emma had blocked that tiny detail from her mind—along with the church, the flowers, the cake and the groom. Most especially the groom. And the kiss from the groom. And the shiver of arousal she got even now when she thought about their engagement kiss on Saturday night.

"If you're going to do this," said Mrs. Nash. "And let me go on record here and now as being dead set *against* your doing this. For the sake of the family, you're going to do it right."

"We can do it right without Amelia's dress," said Alex.

"You definitely don't want Cassandra's." Mrs. Nash spoke to Emma. "Or Rosalind's."

"I was thinking of something from Ferragamo or Vera Wang," said Alex.

"New?" asked Mrs. Nash with obvious horror.

"What's wrong with Cassandra and Rosalind's dresses?" asked Emma, partly to appease Mrs. Nash, but also partly to put Alex in his place. If he thought he was picking out her wedding dress, he had another think coming.

"Rosalind died young, dear."

"Oh, I'm so—"

"It was in nineteen-forty-two," Alex put in.

"Oh." Okay. So maybe condolences weren't necessary.

"And Cassandra." Mrs. Nash clicked her tongue. "She was a most unhappy child." She cast a knowing look at Alex. "And you two have quite enough problems without the dubious karma of that dress."

"It's a very generous offer," Emma said to Mrs. Nash. "But I'm sure I can find something on Fifth—"

"Do you want the world to believe you're marrying for love?"

Emma hesitated, thinking of poor Princess Diana. "We do."

Mrs. Nash divided her disdain between both of them. "I must say, if I'm to be a coconspirator in this folly, then you will have to take my advice."

Emma almost said *yes, ma'am.*

"A Garrison," Mrs. Nash continued, "would never buy a wedding dress off the rack. Now, let's take a look at the ring, shall we?"

Alex slanted an accusatory glare at Emma, and she guiltily inched her hands behind her back.

"I, uh, left it at home."

"Indeed." But then, instead of leveling a criticism, Mrs. Nash gave a decisive nod. "Just as well. We'll be needing the Tudor diamond for this."

Emma didn't know what the Tudor diamond was, but it sounded old and sentimental, and most certainly valuable. She shook her head. "I don't want any of Alex's heirlooms."

"But of course you do."

"No, really—"

Alex slipped an arm around her shoulder. "Mrs. Nash is right, Emma."

She shook her head more vigorously, fighting the reaction to his touch. Why did this stupid sensation have to rise up every time he put his hands on her? It was beyond frustrating, and it made no sense whatsoever.

Sure, he was a fit, sexy man who smelled like cedar musk. And he was rich and smart, with a brilliant if convoluted set of ethics that she couldn't help but admire.

And he sometimes seemed to have her best interests at heart. And every once in a while he showed a soft spot or a wicked streak of humor. She liked that. She didn't want to, but there was no point in denying he could make her laugh.

"You need to save those for your real bride," she insisted.

"That would be you," said Mrs. Nash. "*You* are his real bride."

"No, I'm…" She turned to Alex for support.

He shrugged his shoulders, and she felt completely adrift. The heirloom ring, on top of everything else, suddenly seemed ridiculously overwhelming.

"We need to get organized," Emma told him. Maybe if they made a list—the prenup, the ceremony, where they'd live, how long they had to stay together. Maybe then she'd feel like things were under control.

"Exactly," Mrs. Nash agreed. "And we'll begin with the Tudor diamond. It's being stored in the safe in the Wiltshire bedroom. I trust you remember the combination, Alex?"

"I remember the combination, Mrs. Nash."

"Well, we're not keeping the liquor in there, so you won't have had a use for it lately."

"I should have fired you years ago," said Alex, but there was clear affection in his tone.

Their banter made Emma feel even more like an interloper. "I'm sure the ring isn't intended—"

"You might take a look through the rest of the collection while you're up there," Mrs. Nash added. Then she winked at Alex. "Nothing says commitment quite like flawless emeralds."

Alex nodded to Mrs. Nash and patted Emma's shoulder. "Shall we?"

No, they shouldn't. She had to slow this thing

down. They *had* to get organized. "We need to talk," she said with renewed vigor.

"We can talk in the Wiltshire bedroom."

Six

"**Y**ou'll definitely have to write these into the prenup." Perched on the edge of the four-poster bed, Emma had given up trying to reason with Alex. Instead, she slid a serpentine pattern ruby-and-diamond choker over her forearm. She'd have to be blind not to appreciate the brilliance of the jewels against her pale skin. A more mercenary person might be plotting ways to keep the necklace.

McKinley Inns had certainly allowed Emma and Katie to grow up with a lot of advantages in life, but it was still a relatively small company, and there'd been lean times with their family business. It was hard to imagine a threat to the Garrison wealth. Alex had produced an emerald necklace that looked to be a hundred years old. And she could only guess at the fortune tucked away in the leather and velvet boxes of the multi-shelved safe.

Alex extracted yet another case from a high shelf. "Would that be in favor of you or me?"

"I'm an option?" she joked. "Because a girl could get attached to some of these things."

So far, they'd discovered a sapphire pendant, several diamond bracelets, a man's ruby ring, even a tiara dripping with so many teardrop diamonds that Emma was sure it should be in a museum.

Still, the serpentine choker outshone them all.

"Afraid I can only lend them to you." He smiled at her as he crossed the room, his eyes going a shade of smoke she was beginning to like. "But we'll say yes to some of the party invitations, so you can show them off."

"Only if we bring along a bodyguard." She'd be scared to death wearing the necklace in public.

"You don't need a bodyguard." He waggled his eyebrows. "You've got me."

She couldn't help but grin at that one. "Okay.

But only if you bring along great-great-great Grandpa Hamilton's saber."

"You don't think it might attract attention?"

"I thought attracting attention to us was your mission in life."

He snapped open the newly discovered case. "Touché."

"I, on the other hand." She gave in to temptation and looped the heavy choker around her neck. "Am trying to be classy and circumspect about our engagement."

Alex set the case down on the edge of the bed, motioning for her to turn around. "Let me."

Emma stood and faced away from him so that he could work with the clasp.

He brushed her hair out of the way and took the two ends from her fingertips.

"Thanks," she whispered, allowing herself a few seconds to enjoy the brush of his hands and the fan of his breath.

He smoothed the necklace and touched her shoulders, half turning her so she was facing a big oval mirror above a mahogany vanity table. "Take a look."

Emma's hand went to her throat where the

necklace sparkled with the brilliance of two dozen flawless gems. She took a few steps closer, watching the diamonds reflect the light and the heavy gold glisten with her movements.

"Stunning," she breathed out loud.

"Stunning," Alex agreed, his voice a low rumble.

She glanced up and met his eyes in the mirror. The smoky gray had turned to dark slate. His gaze dropped to the necklace, and in slow motion he brushed away a few stray strands of her hair.

Then he leaned down.

She knew she should stop him. She *had* to stop him. But her body was already anticipating the taste of his lips, his smooth warm lips against the delicate curve of her neck. Desire sizzled within her, and she held still, waiting, wanting.

His lips touched her skin, nudging the necklace out of the way, drawing her in with a gentle kiss. Her hands grasped the vanity top, steadying herself as her need for him took the strength out of her knees.

He broke contact, but then kissed her again. This time the tip of his tongue drew a circle above her collarbone. He blew on the moist spot, and her entire body contracted in response. Then he moved to the other side of her neck with a full, enveloping, overwhelming kiss.

Higher, then higher still. He kissed her jawline, her cheek, then his hands tunneled into her hair, bringing her head around as he zeroed in on her mouth.

When his lips met hers, passion and longing welled up from every corner of her being. She released the vanity, grasping his arm instead, clinging to the strength of his bicep and turning fully into his embrace.

While one hand guided her chin, his free arm snaked around her waist, pulling her firmly into the cradle of his thighs. His muscles were hot and hard as steel, transmitting the unmistakable signals of male desire.

His mouth opened wide, and she answered greedily. His tongue plundered her inviting depths, sending pulsating messages of need through her veins. She subconsciously arched her spine, moving closer, pressing her pelvis, her breasts, her thighs tight against his body.

The world outside disappeared, and her only thought was Alex. His incredible scent, his unbridled power, and the salty, tangy, heady taste of his skin fueled her hunger and hijacked any semblance of reason.

"Emma." Her name vibrated on his lips.

His hand slid to her bottom, grinding her high and tight against him, leaving her no illusions about the state of his arousal. The knowledge shot through her, ricocheting out from the apex of her thighs, streaking electricity to her toes and fingertips.

She cupped his face, smoothing her palms over his rough, masculine skin. She dug her fingers into his hair, kissing him harder, kissing him deeper. There was a primal magic to this passion, something she'd never, ever felt before.

In some dim recess of her mind, she knew they'd have to stop. But not now, not yet.

His breathing grew ragged. With both hands, he lifted her from the floor, slipping her skirt up her thighs, wrapping her legs around his waist so that the fabric of his suit abraded the thin silk of her panties. His thumbs slipped beneath the delicate elastic, and her muscles clenched around the touch.

Alex swore under his breath.

Emma couldn't disagree.

"We have to stop," he groaned.

She nodded, not sure she was capable of forming words.

His thumbs circled higher, forcing a moan from her lips.

"Don't do that," he growled.

"Then stop—" She moaned again.

His hands retreated. He drew his head back to gaze into her eyes. "I want you," he confessed bluntly, then waited for her reaction.

She took a breath. Then another. Then another, desperately gathering her bearings. "That can't be good."

"On the contrary," he said as he slowly lowered her to the floor. "I have a feeling it could be very, very good."

She moved away, out of range, shaking her head. "Don't you say that."

"Not saying it won't change a thing."

Maybe not, but it was all she had. She couldn't take this. She'd never felt so wickedly free, as if some unbridled hedonist had taken over her body. She would have said anything, promised anything, *done* anything.

"We can't ever do it again," she murmured.

"That's one solution," he agreed. But then his voice dipped low, and he leaned slightly forward. "Or else we do, do it again. But we never, ever stop."

The room temperature seemed to spike as they stared at each other. For a moment, Emma actually hesitated over the choice.

Abrupt noises came from the other side of the bedroom door.

"*Mr.* Garrison," Mrs. Nash cried from the hallway.

Her rapid footsteps were followed by more measured ones and a litany of rapid-fire French.

"Philippe," said Emma as Alex reflexively sprang toward the door.

It burst open, and Mrs. Nash marched inside.

"Will you *please* be so kind as to inform this odious man that the Garrison wedding feast dates back to William the Conqueror, and that we are *not* serving Garrison guests microscopic portions of bottom-feeding crustaceans smothered in outlandish butter sauces while I'm alive and breathing." She took a breath.

"A slab of beef and a dollop of dough?"

Philippe demanded, coming abreast of Mrs. Nash. "You have the nerve to call that food?"

"I call that the Queen's supper," Mrs. Nash snapped in return.

"You Brits don't know how to do anything but *boil.*"

"I'll boil you, you——-"

"*Excuse* me?" Alex interrupted, glancing back and forth between the two.

Philippe seemed to recover his composure. "Forgive me, Mr. Garrison. Mademoiselle." He clicked his heels together and fixed his attention on Alex. "I am Philippe Gagnon. Sous Chef, trained at the Sorbonne and apprenticed under John-Pierre Laconte. I have cooked for princes and presidents. And I am at your service."

Alex turned to blink at Emma.

"I hired a caterer," she confessed into the silence.

He paused, his expression carefully neutral. "You hired a caterer?"

"Is that a bad thing?" Before the question was out, she knew it sounded ridiculous. Mrs. Nash was about to call up the Royal Navy. And Philippe's complexion was turning an unnatural shade of purple.

Alex didn't answer, but his eyes widened.

Mrs. Nash sniffed. "You *are* the bride, of course."

Emma might be the bride, but it was easy to see she'd stepped on some very important toes. She hadn't wanted to hire a caterer. It had been an act of self-preservation.

Though she had to admit, Philippe was wonderful. He'd cleared her lobby and emptied her mezzanine of unwanted wedding planners and reporters. Since then, he'd been nothing but professional and helpful. She didn't want to fire him.

But Mrs. Nash, who was obviously the uncontested mistress of her domain had very concrete plans for Alex's wedding. Emma sure didn't want to alienate her, either.

She glanced at Alex. No help there. He was obviously waiting for her next move.

She looked from Mrs. Nash to Philippe and back again. "Could we, um, compromise?" she asked.

Alex coughed. "You want the English and the French to compromise over food?"

"Is that a bad thing, too?"

No one seemed inclined to answer.

"I am willing," Philippe finally put in, with a long-suffering sigh, "to make a few—how do you say—concessions."

Emma glanced hopefully at Mrs. Nash.

Mrs. Nash's lips pursed.

"Mrs. Nash?" Alex prompted.

"It's tradition," she spouted.

Emma struggled to come up with something helpful. "Perhaps you could do the main course? And Philippe could do dessert?"

"Mon Dieu." Philippe crossed himself. "I will be ruined."

Mrs. Nash clacked her teeth together. "The admiral would turn over in his grave."

Emma looked to Alex once more. He should feel free to jump in anytime.

"Any more good ideas?" he asked her.

That did it. This whole mess was his fault anyway. "*You* were the one who proposed in public. You unleashed the dogs."

"What dogs?"

"Philippe is the one who saved me. He cleared out the reporters. He sent the other caterers packing—"

"Thirty-five years," Mrs. Nash put in. "Thirty-five years I've been with the Garrison family."

Philippe made a slashing motion with his hand. "Yorkshire pudding and boiled cabbage has *no place* on my table."

"*Your* table?" cried Mrs. Nash. "I think you mean Mr. Garrison's table."

"Can we get back to the dogs?" asked Alex.

"They were metaphorical," said Emma.

"I got that much," he drawled.

"The press," said Philippe, providing a few more dramatic hand gestures. "They were everywhere. Ms. McKinley was forced into hiding. I saved her."

"He saved me," Emma agreed. And she wasn't about to fire the man for his trouble. Surely to goodness four sane adults could come up with a compromise.

She turned to Mrs. Nash. "Why don't we pull out your recipes—"

"Water, salt and a big ol' slab of beef," said Philippe.

"At least it's not the legs of amphibians—"

"That's it." Alex took a decisive step forward. "Philippe, Mrs. Nash, you'll work together. I want three recommendations for a compromise by Wednesday."

The two immediately stopped talking.

"Morning," said Alex.

After a pause, Philippe and Mrs. Nash eyed each other suspiciously.

"Can I get a yes?" Alex prompted.

Philippe lifted his chin. "But of course. I will do everything in my power to assist."

"We can certainly discuss it," said Mrs. Nash, canting her chin at an equally challenging angle.

"Then, thank you," said Alex. "If you'll excuse us, Emma and I were picking out some jewelry."

Both Philippe and Mrs. Nash nodded stiffly and exited the room. Mrs. Nash closed the door behind them.

Alex gave Emma an exaggerated sigh of exhaustion. "A Frenchman?"

"How was I supposed to know you had a rabid housekeeper?"

Alex ambled back to the open safe. "You're right. Silly me. Anything else I should know about? A Greek limousine driver? A Romanian florist?"

"What does Mrs. Nash have against the Romanians?"

His back was to her, but Emma could tell Alex smiled at that.

"Maybe you should run any future plans by me first."

"To pander to your control freakish nature?"

"To avoid murder or dismemberment during the ceremony. Ahhh. Here it is."

Emma's curiosity got the better of her, and she stepped closer to the safe. "What did you find in there?"

He popped open a purple velvet box. "The Tudor diamond."

Emma glanced down at the jewel in his hands and instantly stopped breathing.

It was gorgeous.

Old, unique, luxuriant and gorgeous.

The band was fashioned from strands of platinum, woven together to form an intricate Celtic pattern. Rubies tapered up the curve, highlighting the centerpiece—a glittering oval of a flawless gem.

The Tudor diamond.

"Try it on," said Alex.

She shook her head. Fake brides didn't touch a piece like that. At the very least, it had to be bad luck.

He moved the box toward her. "Mrs. Nash is right. The family jewels work in our favor."

Emma shook again, shifting from one foot to the other, her heart rate increasing. No way. No how. The ring he'd given her at casino night was perfectly fine.

"It is insured," he said.

"Against bad luck?"

He glanced at the ring in confusion. "What bad luck? It's nothing but metal and stone."

"It's a precious family heirloom."

"And it's my family heirloom. And I want you to wear it."

"That's not your choice to make."

Alex frowned. "It is my choice. I own the ring. I own the collection, the safe, the house. And I can give them to any damn person I please."

She couldn't do it. She just couldn't do it. "I'm talking morality, not legality."

The frustration in his voice was obvious. "How is it immoral for you to wear my ring?"

"Because I'd be disrespecting all the brides who came before me."

Alex blinked. Then he squinted, and a funny little smile flexed his face. "Emma. Do you honestly think you're the first Garrison bride to marry for money?"

Emma wasn't marrying for money. At least not the way he was insinuating she was marrying for money. She had her own money. He was simply… Well, he was helping her out, for a handsome return, that was all.

It was mutually beneficial, and she resented him making her feel otherwise.

"This has been going on since the early eighteen-hundreds," said Alex. "Even my father—" Then he clamped his jaw. "Hold out your hand, Emma."

She started to retreat, but he reached out and snagged her left wrist, coaxing it toward him.

"I don't—"

He slipped the band over her first knuckle.

She shut her mouth and stared at the endless circle of platinum, at Alex's dark hand against her own pale skin, at the antique rubies and diamond winking in the light.

"Believe me when I tell you," said Alex, pushing it a little farther. "You're carrying on a proud tradition."

The ring thudded reluctantly over her second knuckle, but then it settled at the base of her finger.

A perfect fit.

"There," Alex breathed, stroking his thumb over the surface of the diamond. "Now we're really engaged."

Where Alex had ended up with Hamilton's fortune and Hamilton's looks, his third cousin, Nathaniel, had ended up with Hamilton's life. The second son of the current earl of Kessex, Nathaniel had been forced to seek his own fortune, just as Hamilton had done so many decades before.

With little more than seed money from the family estate, Nathaniel had founded Kessex Cruise Lines. Then he'd added Kessex Shipping and quickly grew his fortune to the hundreds of millions.

He now had his finger on the pulse of the transportation industry from Paris to Auckland. And the transportation industry was the lynchpin of global commerce. Alex might know how to run a successful hotel chain. But Nathaniel could manipulate the world.

He'd provided Alex with a thick dossier on DreamLodge, then he'd hung around an extra couple of days. He should have been on his way back to London today. His continued presence made Alex nervous. Nathaniel didn't stick around unless something was interesting. And things that Nathaniel found interesting usually made Alex sweat.

The two men, along with Ryan, waited until Simone exited and closed the door to Alex's office.

"What's going on?" Alex asked his cousin without preamble.

Across the round meeting table, Nathaniel inched slightly forward in his chair. "You ever met David Cranston?"

That sure wasn't what Alex had expected to hear. "You mean Katie McKinley's boyfriend?"

Nathaniel nodded.

"Sure," said Alex.

Nathaniel strummed a single staccato beat with his fingertips. "He's on my radar."

Ryan jumped in. "Why?"

Nathaniel's mood became contemplative. "Don't know yet."

"Gut feeling?" asked Alex, knowing the answer already.

Nathaniel's gut feeling was legendary in the family. He made million-dollar deals based on nothing but a vague shimmer of a theory.

His uncanny luck used to freak Alex out. But then Nathaniel explained his luck was, in fact, the sum total of several hundred subconscious observations, from facial expressions and stock trends to weather patterns and newspaper articles. He wasn't sure himself how it worked. He only knew that it did.

The phenomenon didn't freak Alex out anymore, and he'd quit calling it luck years ago.

"Gut feeling," Nathaniel confirmed. "Did you know McKinley Inns just hired him?"

"Cranston?" asked Alex, more than slightly bothered that he had to hear news like that from his cousin. "Doing what?"

"Overseas marketing. VP Special Projects."

Ryan snorted. "*Special* projects?"

"Pathetic," Nathaniel agreed.

"What's his background?" asked Alex. And what was Emma thinking?

Nathaniel shrugged. "Some kind of mediocre project manager for Leon Gage Consulting."

"Did they can him?"

Nathaniel shook his head. "He quit."

"McKinley actually headhunted him?"

Nathaniel nodded. "Offered him a salary bump."

"The guy's a mooch," said Ryan. "Takes a cushy job with the girlfriend's firm…"

Alex hated the thought of McKinley Inns supporting a do-nothing executive, particularly where nepotism was involved.

Then again he wasn't stupid enough to get between his fiancée's sister and her true love, either. Of all the battles he wanted to take on at McKinley, this sure wasn't on the top of his list.

Nathaniel stood up. "That's all I wanted to tell you."

Alex stood with his cousin. "You're offended on an ethical level, aren't you?"

"Nothing worse than a wussie who rides on his woman's coattails. You should have a talk with this Katie person. Tell her to dump the bastard."

Alex scoffed out a laugh. "Right. Like that's going to happen."

"She's got rotten taste in men."

"She's also got fifty acres of beachfront property on Kayven Island. She can marry her St. Bernard for all I care."

Nathaniel gave him a mock two-fingered salute. "Thanks for the visual there, Al."

"Not a problem, Nate. Everything still on track for the Kayven Island project?"

"Minor problem with the dockworkers' union, but I straightened it out. Everything still on track at your end?"

"Absolutely." Emma had a ring on her finger, and they'd had very positive coverage in three major newspapers.

Nathaniel slid his chair back under the meeting table. "In that case, gentlemen. I've got a girl and a plane both waiting on the tarmac at JFK."

Alex reached out and shook Nathaniel's hand. "Thanks for the intel. On both fronts."

"Anytime." Then Nathaniel nodded to Ryan. "Catch you later."

Ryan rose to his feet. "Have a good flight."

Nathaniel grinned and turned for the door,

tossing his parting words over his shoulder. "Plane's my new Learjet Sixty. Girl's a licensed masseuse from Stockholm."

Alex crossed to his desk as the door clicked shut behind Nathaniel. "Guess he *will* be having a good flight."

"How do I get his life?" asked Ryan.

"Most people want his brother's."

Wednesday evening, Katie grasped at the unwieldy ring on Emma's left hand. *"No way,"* she exclaimed.

"Way," said Emma, still struggling to get used to the weight of the thing and still worrying about the insurance implications if she lost it.

Katie looked up, her eyes shining under the lights of Emma's penthouse. "A real earl?"

"About four generations ago."

"Alex *gave you* his family heirloom?"

"Don't go getting all excited." Emma liberated her hand and sat back down on the couch. "He's only lending it to me. And it has a dubious history."

Katie took the seat opposite, kicking off her

sandals and curling her feet beneath her. "Oh, do tell."

"The brides all married for money."

Katie stared at her, waiting. "That's it?"

"That's it."

"I thought you were talking about sex and scandal and murder."

"Sorry. No murders." Emma thought back to her afternoon. "Well, except for Mrs. Nash. Alex's housekeeper. I have a feeling she's capable of it."

"And did you upset her?"

"Not so much me. But Philippe better watch his back."

Katie grinned. "I have a feeling Philippe can take care of himself."

Emma had to admit, she had that feeling, too. She stroked her thumb over the big diamond and was assailed by a vivid body memory of Alex. She determinedly shook it off. "So what did I miss at the office?"

Katie tossed her wavy blond hair back over one shoulder. "I got David to come and work for us."

Emma didn't understand. "Your David?"

"Yes, my David."

"But he has a job. With Leon Gage."

"I convinced him to quit."

An uneasy feeling trickled through Emma. "Why would you do that?" David was a great guy. And Katie obviously loved him. But working together? Day in and day out? Could that be good for any couple?

"Because we need him," said Katie, the tone of her voice subtly shifting to petulant.

Emma regrouped.

She wished Katie had discussed it with her. Not that Emma would have overruled her sister, but she might have been able to curb Katie's impulsive nature.

"Did you at least get help from Human Resources?" McKinley had a top notch HR department.

"What? I can marry him, but I can't hire him?"

"Katie—"

"Really, Emma."

Emma clenched her jaw. HR checked references and aligned suitable people with suitable jobs. What would they do if David didn't work out?

Now she struggled to keep the censure out of her voice. "What's he going to do?"

Katie pushed out her bottom lip.

"Katie?"

"Vice President of Special Projects Overseas."

Emma pressed her thumb against the jagged facets of the ring. This time when the memory of Alex popped up, it was strangely comforting. "I see."

"He's got contacts in Europe and all over the Caribbean."

Emma nodded. She wasn't aware they had problems in Europe or the Caribbean.

"He's going after convention business and tour clubs."

Emma couldn't hold her tongue completely. "Are you sure that's not too much togetherness?" She wanted Katie to be happy, truly she did. But there was something about this situation that made her uneasy. For Katie's sake. For the company's.

"You and Alex are going to work together," said Katie.

"But Alex and I aren't—"

"Getting married."

Emma jerked her thumb away from the ring. "Falling in love."

"So? Love makes it easier for me and David to work together."

Emma struggled to find fault with that logic. Technically, she supposed it should be true. Katie and David actually liked and respected each other. Where Alex and Emma couldn't come within ten feet without arguing or...worse.

Fingers spread, Katie raked her blond hair back over her forehead. "Quite frankly, Emma, if you're going to worry about anyone working together, I'd worry about you and Alex."

Emma was already worried about that.

She resisted the urge to touch the ring again.

Quite frankly, she was getting more worried by the hour.

Seven

Emma braced herself for Alex's entrance.

Her admin assistant, Jenny, had just spent three minutes warning of his arrival, an excited lilt to her voice as she watched him walk through the long office foyer and relayed his every move to Emma.

According to Jenny, Alex was wearing a charcoal suit, a black shirt and a silver-and-blue striped tie that picked up the sunshine through the skylights. He didn't look upset, but he didn't look particularly happy either. And, by the way, had Emma ever noticed the delicate cleft in his chin or the way his gray eyes sparkled silver in direct sunlight?

By the time Emma got off the intercom, she only had thirty seconds to smooth her blazer and brace herself for the onslaught of emotions that were sure to be brought on by his presence.

She'd stay on this side of the desk. He'd stay on that side. She wouldn't touch him, or smell him or look too closely into his eyes. And she would not touch that annoying diamond while he was in the room.

The oak door swung open, the air current swaying the leaves on her ponytail palm.

She came to her feet to face not happy, not angry Alex, with his sparkling silver eyes.

"Hello, darling," he greeted for Jenny's benefit before he clicked the door shut behind him.

She drew a bracing breath. "Can I help you with something?" They hadn't made another appointment to meet, although she knew they had an endless number of things to work out.

"Brought you a present."

Please, God. No more jewelry. Her right hand went to the ring before she remembered to jerk it back.

But he tossed an envelope on her desk. "Our prenup."

She glanced at the thick manila envelope. "You wrote it without me?"

He eased down into one of her guest chairs. "Trust me."

"Ha." She peeled back the flap and took her own seat.

It was a single page, duly signed and notarized. Alex got half of McKinley upon their marriage, and if either of them initiated divorce proceedings within two years of the marriage, the other got ten percent of their net worth.

She looked up to see him smile. There wasn't a single thing she could complain about. It meant she couldn't have a relationship for a couple of years. But she'd expected that. If anything, the agreement favored her.

Then she set the paper down on her desk. "What exactly is your net worth?"

"Less than Nathaniel's. More than yours."

"Who's Nathaniel?"

"My cousin. He'll be the best man."

She glanced back down at the agreement. "You've already signed."

"I have."

"You're obviously not planning to divorce me anytime soon."

"Not a chance."

Emma picked up her phone and dialed the two-digit extension for Jenny's desk. "Can you bring somebody over from Legal?"

"Right away," Jenny confirmed.

"Thanks." Emma hung up the phone. "Probably be about five minutes," she told Alex.

He nodded. "I hear you hired David Cranston."

"Where'd you hear that?"

Alex shrugged. "I told you the hotel business was a tight-knit community."

"Katie hired him," said Emma, then she immediately regretted the admission.

"Without talking to you?"

Emma hesitated. "We talked."

"You're lying."

"I am not. And how dare you—"

"And you agreed to this?"

Emma compressed her lips.

Alex stared hard into her eyes. Despite her resolve, and despite the knowledge that she'd ramp up her unruly hormones, she gazed right back into his.

"She told you after the fact," he guessed.

"But I wouldn't have stopped her."

"But you don't like it."

Emma stood up. "No," she admitted, pacing toward the picture window. "I don't like it. But it's her relationship, her decision. And it's certainly none of your business."

Alex stood. "Oh, yes it is."

She turned. "You going to micromanage Katie's staff?"

"He's working directly *for* her?"

"Alex."

Alex crossed the room to stand in front of Emma. "Between the two of us—"

"No," she barked.

"You don't even know what I was going to say."

Anger rising, she punctuated her words by poking him in the chest with her index finger. "Oh yes I do. And don't you ever *dare* suggest that we gang up on my sister. McKinley Inns doesn't work that way. I don't care who the hell you are."

He trapped her hand. "It's a bad decision."

"It's *her* decision."

"And you're just going to stand there and watch her make it."

"I am. And so are you."

He moved closer. "I wouldn't be too quick to tell me what I am and am not going to do."

Emma paused. She couldn't force him. But then he couldn't force her either. And a tie went to the status quo. Which meant the tie went to Katie in this case.

Emma didn't smile, but she came close.

But then she became aware of Alex's hand on hers. The warmth of his skin prickled its way into her bloodstream, and those appalling feelings of lust and longing surged to life inside her.

His voice dropped deep and throaty. "We're going to have to deal with it, you know."

"With Katie?" she asked in a small voice, clinging to the slim hope that that's what he meant.

"With the fact that we turn each other on like original sin."

"We do not," she lied.

"Want me to prove it?"

She tried to step back, but he kept hold of her hand.

He smiled. "You really need to stop lying to me, you know."

"You really need to develop some manners."

"Yeah? Okay, how's this? Would you care to accompany me to a luau?"

"A luau?" The sudden switch left Emma's head spinning.

"Kessex Cruise Lines is launching a new ship, the *Island Countess,* specializing in Polynesian trips. We're invited to the launch party, and I thought you could wear the ruby-and-diamond choker."

Emma had already resigned herself to being seen in public with Alex. She'd made a deal, and she was going to stick by it. Besides, being with him in public was quickly becoming a preferable choice to being with him in private.

In public she could pretend she was still pretending. She'd have an excuse to talk to Alex and laugh with Alex and touch Alex without examining the reasons why.

Doing those things in private forced her to admit she liked him. She even liked arguing with him. His self-confidence and strength of purpose made her feel...safe somehow.

And she trusted him. Probably not the smartest move in the world. But she had to trust somebody. And he was learning things about her that nobody else would ever see.

For now, for this moment in time, he was pivotal to her life. Not that she'd admit that to him. And not that she'd make things easy.

"You really think rubies and diamonds will go with orchid print cotton?" she asked.

"Hey, you want to look good or make your future husband happy?"

"Can't I do both?"

"Not in this case."

They stared each other down for a long minute.

"Well?" he demanded.

She tilted her head sideways. "Don't you sometimes wish you'd picked the pretty one?"

"Watch it."

"Watch what?" She was only joking. Besides, it was an acknowledged fact that Katie was the pretty one.

"Mess with me, and I'll make you admit I turn you on."

"How do you plan—"

His eyes darkened and his nostrils flared.

She quickly backtracked. "Never mind." Then she swallowed and squared her shoulders, voice going unnaturally sweet. "I *live* to make my future husband happy."

He smiled and brushed her hair back from her temple. "There. Was that so hard? Friday at seven. And I'll bring the necklace."

Climbing the short gangway to the *Island Countess,* Alex told himself everything was fine. He'd expected Emma to be a knockout in her deep-red, Hawaiian-print dress. And he'd expected the Garrison jewels to look stunning against the smooth honey tone of her throat. He'd even expected the sucker-punch sensation he was coming to associate with being in her presence.

What he hadn't expected was his burning desire to keep her all to himself.

Tonight was about parading her for the press, letting the other ladies ooh and ahh over the Tudor diamond on her finger, and solidifying their position as a couple with other players in the New York tourism industry, so that when Alex started representing McKinley, no eyebrows would be raised.

Trouble was, Alex couldn't bring himself to

care about any of those things. There was a steel drum band playing by the pool on the aft sundeck, and all he wanted to do was hold Emma in his arms under the stars.

He knew she hated publicity, but she was doing it anyway. She hated deception, but she'd gone along with his scheme. And she probably hated him, but she was smiling up at him, holding his hand, and plastering her body against his for the benefit of photographer after photographer.

Until now, he hadn't given much thought to how much of a trooper she really was. There was an entire company being saved, her sister, the board, the executives and thousands of jobs. Yet, it was all on Emma's shoulders.

Had she complained?

Of course she had. But she'd made logical, reasonable arguments. She'd looked for options and solutions that would suit her better. But when she didn't find them, when Alex had prevented her from finding them, she'd bucked up and done what was needed.

He admired that.

He admired her.

He motioned to the glass elevator that ran up the five stories of the central atrium.

"Ready to go upstairs?" he whispered against her glistening chestnut hair. He inhaled the scent of her shampoo, his gaze darting to the ruby earrings dangling from her delicate lobes.

His earrings.

He closed his hand over hers, letting the diamond press into his palm.

She leaned up to laugh in his ear. "You think they got enough pictures?"

"Absolutely. Besides, there'll be more photographers on the deck."

She set her empty champagne glass on a waiter's tray. "Then, lead on."

"You're awfully agreeable tonight."

She smiled and waved to a cluster of brightly dressed women. "That's because I live to make you happy."

"Seriously," he said. "You're…" He wasn't quite sure how to put it into words. He finally came up with, "sparkling."

"It's the rubies."

He took the excuse to run his thumb over the

bracelet on her wrist. "They suit you. But that wasn't what I meant."

The elevator door opened in front of them, and they moved inside alone.

"Then it's the champagne," she said, bracing her hands on the small railing and leaning back against the glass wall.

The posture brought the cotton fabric tight against her breasts, and Alex felt his body involuntarily take note. The dress was strapless and fitted, with a tie cinching up the waist and a narrow skirt delineating her hips before falling softly to just above her knees.

Most of the women had gone with island styles, the men sticking with casual slacks and open-collar shirts. Alex had gone with tan and buff, not being a fan of wearing palm fronds across his chest.

From the shine of her soft hair to the tips of her painted toenails, Emma looked like an island goddess.

"Are you drunk?" he asked. That might account for her relaxed mood.

She eased away from the wall, moving sinuously toward him, stopping to walk her fingertips up his chest and grasp the small lapels of his shirtfront. She shook her hair and gazed slumberously up into his eyes. "I'm acting, Alex. I thought that was what you were paying me for."

He leaned down ever so slightly. "Well, you're very, very good."

She smiled.

"Almost too good."

Her expression faltered. "What's that supposed to—"

The door glided open to some new passengers, and he slipped his arm around her narrow waist. "Let's dance."

Without waiting for a response, he drew her into his arms, and they joined dozens of other couples under the stars, swaying to the calypso beat.

Her movements matched his, stiff at first, but then she found his rhythm. He snuggled her closer, pressing her hips to his thighs. She was just the right size, just the right shape, just the right height to be a perfect partner.

His thoughts turned to movements of a sexual nature, speculating on how perfect things could be between them. Of course, he was only talking about sex, not about life. Life with Emma was going to be a challenge from the minute he got up in the morning to the minute he went to bed at night.

Alone.

Because their marriage wasn't about intimacy. It was about convenience. And for the first time, Alex wondered if Mrs. Nash might be right. He didn't really like the thought of a cold, lonely death.

Nor did he like the thought of a cold, lonely bed. In fact, he didn't like the thought of a bed with anyone in it but Emma at the moment.

Which was impossible, in so many ways.

But she was in his arms now.

He closed his eyes and gathered her to him, tipping his head to the crook of her neck, inhaling her scented skin and letting the smooth, warmed gems of her necklace rub against his cheek. A camera flash penetrated his lids. And even though it was what he wanted, he resented the intrusion.

He danced Emma to a quieter corner of the ship's deck, where the lights were dim and the music was muted by wind baffles.

She tilted back her head and stared at the panorama of stars above them. "A romantic tryst for the press?"

"Something like that." He focused on the smooth skin, delicate neck.

She thought they were playacting? What the hell?

He leaned down and feathered a kiss on her collarbone, just below his necklace.

He heard her quick intake of breath, so he tried another one, this time on her shoulders, working his way slowly backward, then up toward the lobe of her ear, which he drew gently into his mouth.

Her fingers dug into his, and he splayed his hand wide on the small of her back, bringing her tight against him as his mouth sought hers.

Their bodies knew each other's this time. There was no fumbling, not the slightest hesitation. Their lips met full on. Their mouths opened. And their tongues parried in a way that sent sparks shooting straight to Alex's groin.

This was a bad idea.

No. This was a great idea. What it was, was a bad location for a great idea.

They were screened from the crowd at the moment, but that could change. All it would take is one rogue reporter or one straying couple, and they'd be caught in a compromising position.

Not that he'd compromised her yet.

He was only kissing her.

But judging by her quiet moans, and the way his hand was inching down her bottom, it was only a matter of minutes.

He dragged himself back.

She blinked in confusion, her lips red and swollen, her eyes clouded with passion.

"I want to show you something," he whispered.

He led her past the deck chairs, through an airlock door, up a small staircase to the Empress Deck and the door to a vista suite. There he inserted the card key.

"What's this?" she asked.

He opened the narrow door. "The captain thought we might like to freshen up."

Emma walked inside, glancing around at the dining table, the sofa cluster and wet bar. "But there are no reporters in here." She looked back at Alex in confusion.

Had she really been acting the whole time?

He couldn't believe it.

"The veranda," he quickly improvised. "It overlooks the party."

He crossed the spacious room and pressed a button to pull back the drapes. He'd back off from the seduction plan. Really, nothing ventured nothing gained.

The drapes slid out of the way to reveal a huge, wraparound veranda with views of the portside pool, the ocean and the New York skyline.

He opened the two French doors, letting in the night air and calypso music and party laughter. "Nothing like a clandestine telephoto lens shot to convince people we're in love."

Emma peered through the doorway at the crowds dancing one deck below. "You're frighteningly conniving, you know that?"

He reached for her hand, muttering under his breath. "You don't know the half of it." Then louder. "Shall we get cozy on the double lounger?"

She stepped outside on her strappy sandals, her dress billowing gently around shapely legs. "Why not. You think they'd bring us up one of those pineapple drinks?"

"You got it," said Alex, picking up the phone to push the button for the butler.

Emma felt much safer out on the veranda than inside the suite with Alex. She'd thought, planned, *hoped* to spend the entire evening in a crowd of people. And she sure hadn't counted on Alex going for quite so much realism. Those kisses had all but sizzled her toes.

When she thought about it though, it made perfect sense. A newly engaged couple wouldn't stay in the thick of the party all night long. They'd steal away for a kiss or two in private. Letting the press spot them on the suite's veranda was inspired.

She sat down on the thick padding of the double lounger and kicked off the tight high heels she'd borrowed from Katie. The dress was Katie's, too. While Emma was well outfitted for business events, she'd never built up her party and vacation wardrobe. Luckily, she and Katie were the same size.

Alex set a tall, frosted glass on the mini table beside her. "One frozen Wiki Waki."

"You made that up."

He held up a hand. "Swear it's true. That's what they're serving at the party."

The frost slipped against Emma's fingers as she lifted the glass and stirred the mixture with the straw. It was crisp and tangy on her tongue, and the blend of liquors definitely left an afterglow.

The cushion shifted as Alex sat down.

"What have you got?" she asked.

"Glenroddich on the rocks."

"Wrong hemisphere."

He leaned back and closed his eyes. "That's as exotic as I get."

She smirked, wiggling her bare toes in the cool ocean breeze. "I knew you'd be a dud as soon as I saw the outfit."

He opened one eye. "You messing with me again?"

She took another sip of the tropical drink. "I'm merely entertaining myself while we pose for the photographers."

"By playing mind games with me?"

"Afraid I'll win?"

He snorted and closed his eyes again. "Afraid you might sprain something trying."

Emma glanced at his slacks, then she glanced at her slushy drink.

He made a show of settling back to a more comfortable position. "But, go ahead and give it your best shot."

"Really?" she simpered. "Can I?"

He grinned, and she upended her drink in his lap.

He shot up straight, his roar loud enough to attract attention from the dancers directly below them. Then he turned to stare at her in horror.

"That was my best shot," she explained, scrambling for the courage to hold her ground. Dousing him had seemed like a good idea about ten seconds ago. Now...

"I can't believe you did that." He gritted his teeth as the sticky peach-colored mixture trickled between his thighs.

"You might want to make it look like we're having fun," she suggested with a quick glance at the crowd below.

Alex curved his mouth into a pained grin. "You asked for this."

Without further warning, he scooped her up,

and sat her square in the middle of the mess on his lap.

"It's Katie's dress," she shrieked. Then she cringed as the ice seeped through her panties.

His fingertips went to her ribs, and she shrieked a second time when he started tickling. "Don't," she gasped. "Stop."

"Don't stop?"

"No. Stop!"

"Try to sound like you're having fun," he advised.

"No." But she kept laughing. She couldn't help it. She wasn't sure where he'd learned to tickle, but he was definitely a master.

"Help," she called weakly to the crowd below.

But they couldn't hear her over the music.

Alex's hands suddenly stilled, but it was only to lift her from the lounger and carry her unceremoniously back through the French doors.

He set her down and closed it to the whoops and hollers of those below.

"What did I tell you?" he asked, eyes flashing dark and purposeful in the dusky suite.

"About what?" She took an involuntary step backward.

He matched her pace, keeping the distance constant between them. "About messing with me, that's about what."

His meaning hit, and she scooted up against the wall. "Oh, no." She shook her head.

He moved forward, trapping her between the sofa and the wet bar. "Oh, yes," he said menacingly. "It's a matter of pride now."

Her glance darted to his ruined trousers. "You already got me back." Her dress was just as wet as his pants.

He shook his head. "Not good enough. Admit I turn you on, Emma."

She knew she should say it. She should say it and get it over with. He'd make good on his threat, that was for sure. And ten kisses from now, she'd be admitting the earth was flat and that she was a witch, never mind that he turned her on.

But she shook her head anyway. She couldn't bring herself to go down without a fight. He might get her admission, but he was going to have to work for it.

He moved even closer, his voice instantly seductive. "You know I'll do it."

She nodded.

"You *want* me to do it?"

She shook.

He raised his hand and tenderly stroked his palm over her cheek, tangling his fingers into the hair behind her temple. "You think you have a hope in hell?"

She stared defiantly up at him. "I know I have a hope in hell."

He cracked a half smile. "Just one?"

"Maybe two."

"I do like those odds."

She almost smiled in return and wondered why she wasn't more wary of the situation. Maybe it was his soothing tone, or his reassuring strength or his comforting scent. Or maybe it was because she was looking forward to his kiss.

His kiss? Who was she kidding?

She was looking forward to anything and everything he'd do before she said uncle. Confidence mounting, she stared directly into his slate dark eyes. "Go ahead, Alex. Give it your best shot."

Eight

Alex went still, his eyes narrowing as he stared down at Emma. "Are we playing chicken?" he asked her. "Because it feels like we're playing chicken."

She forced herself to hold her ground. "Are you all talk and no action? Because it feels like you're—"

He swooped down and enveloped her mouth in a hot, passionate kiss. His strong arms held her protectively, lovingly. Sensations racked her body as the damp of his slacks seeped through to her dress. His tongue flicked out, and his fingers anchored firmly at the base of her neck.

The room spun, even as her world came to a full stop.

Okay. Now *that* was action.

"Say it," he rumbled.

She shook her head, no.

His hand moved to her rib cage, stroking upward to engulf her breast. Through the thin cotton fabric, his thumb unerringly zeroed in on her nipple, circling it once then abrading the tip.

Her body was instantly flooded with desire.

"Say you want me," he tried again.

She locked her knees to keep them from buckling but refused to concede the test of wills.

"Have it your way," he muttered, kissing her once more.

She tasted the mellow, nutty flavor of his scotch, inhaled the heady scent of his musk then felt his warm fingertips creep beneath her neckline. He inched his way closer, closer, closer still. Until she arched her back, pushing her aching breast into his hot hand.

He groaned in response, assuaging her nipple with an expert motion. Goose bumps rose on her skin. Her body clamored for more.

What was he doing?

He did it again, and she cried out loud.

"Say it," he hissed, his mouth brushing against hers.

She whimpered a no.

He swore under his breath.

Then he scooped her up into his arms and carried her through the narrow doorway, depositing her on the thick comforter of the king-sized bed.

Before she had time to breathe, he bent over her, staring into her eyes as he released the tie of her wraparound dress. Silver flecks smoldered in the depths of black slate as he eased the dress open, revealing her cleavage, her navel, the lace front of her panties.

His breathing grew ragged. "Just say it, Emma."

She reached beneath his shirt, running her fingers up his chest, through the sparse hair and over the flat of his nipples, giving back at least some of what she was getting.

He trapped her wrist. "Me wanting you was never the question."

Right. Damn.

He slowly released her, sending his own fingertips on a sensual journey between her breasts, over her stomach, dipping ever lower. He touched the detailed top of her panties. Then he traced a line over the translucent fabric, zigzagging across her sensitive flesh, before stopping and cupping her, rubbing the heel of his hand on the center of her passion.

With his free hand, he separated her dress, exposing her naked breasts. His eyes feasted on her pale skin and her pink, tightly contracted nipples as her chest rose and fell with labored breathing.

He kissed one nipple, laving it with his tongue, pulling it into a tighter and tighter bud. Then he blew against the damp spot, and she went hot, then cold, then hot all over again.

"All you have to do is say it," he repeated.

In answer, she flexed her hips. His hand was doing such delicious things down there that she didn't think she could speak if she wanted to. And she didn't want to. She didn't want him to win, and she sure didn't want him to stop.

He eased down beside her, burying his face in her neck, planting sharp kisses beside the necklace while he pushed down her panties and sought her warm wet flesh.

She grasped his shoulders, pinching tight as his fingertip found her center. He lingered and circled while her thigh muscles tightened, her toes curled and a small pulse came to life beneath his hand.

"Emma," he gasped, fixing his mouth on hers, plunging his tongue in deep, dragging the dress from her.

He closed a hand over her breast, held it there, then seemed to hold himself back. His eyes were dark as midnight as he gazed down at her. His mouth glistened with moisture, and the dim light from the living room highlighted the planes and angles of his face.

Emma dragged in a lungful of oxygen.

"Either you tell me you want me," he growled, "or I stop right now."

He wouldn't.

He couldn't.

Her inner muscles convulsed with need.

"I want you," she said hoarsely.

"Thank you." His mouth came down on top of hers, and his finger sank inside.

She scrambled with the buttons of his shirt, tearing it apart, holding him tight and pressing her breasts against the roughness of his skin. The heat of his chest seared her even as his mouth found hers, and their tongues began an intimate dance.

Somehow, he kicked off his slacks and located a condom. She raked her fingers through his hair, stroked his stubbled chin, rubbed a finger over his lips and tucked it inside.

He kissed her palm, the inside of her wrist, the crook of her elbow. Then he rose above her and she brought up her knees.

"Emma," he breathed. Trapping her hands, their fingers entwined, he kissed her hard as he plunged to the hilt.

She moaned his name, rising to meet him. The music, the party, the *world* disappeared in a haze of passion as his strokes grew harder and faster and her nerve endings converged on the place where their bodies met.

She closed her eyes as the fireworks pulsed. Small explosions at first. Then they grew higher and brighter and faster until the entire sky erupted in light and color and sound.

"Alex," she cried, and his guttural moan told her he'd followed her off the edge of the earth.

The fireworks slowly ebbed to a glow. The music returned, and the sound of laughter filtered up from the party on the lower deck.

She willed the sounds away. Alex's body was a delicious weight holding her down on the softness of the bed, and she didn't want to surface just yet.

"You okay?" he asked, easing up.

She nodded. "But don't move. For now." She didn't want to break the spell.

"Okay." Then he sighed against her hair. "So nice to know I won."

She tried to work up an appropriate level of indignation, but she was too satiated. "You couldn't give me five minutes, could you?"

"You're a hard nut to crack, Emma McKinley."

"Funny. Here I was thinking I was easy."

His fingers flexed between hers. "Easy? I've never worked so hard for sex in my life."

Okay. The afterglow was officially ebbing. "You can get off now."

He rolled his weight to one side, giving a deep sigh of satisfaction. "You want me."

She bopped him on the shoulder. "Oh, get over yourself."

He held up his hands in mock defense. "I distinctly heard you say it."

"Well, you want me, too."

"Of course I do."

"So, we're even."

He grinned. "Not quite. You don't want to want me. That's not the same thing."

"It was the night," she waxed sarcastically. "The champagne. The cruise ship."

"You telling me this was a shipboard romance?"

"Correct." It had to be. She couldn't go around wanting Alex for the duration of the marriage. The mere thought was…well…unthinkable.

"And it's a very short cruise," she said tartly, sitting up and drawing her dress firmly around her, already regretting having let herself go— with Alex of all people. Talk about taking a complicated situation and blowing it right off the charts.

She glanced around the room. What had she done with her shoes?

Alex sat in silence for a moment, then muttered to himself. "I'll say it was short. We never even left the dock."

"We should go back out to the party," she said.

"Our clothes are covered in Wiki Waki."

Emma made a face.

"I'll call the concierge. I'm sure they can bring us up something we can change into."

And walk back into the party wearing a different dress? "I think I'll hide out here," she stated.

Alex picked up the telephone from the table next to the bed. "Are you kidding? This is perfect."

She turned her head to glare at him. Why were things that were so perfect for him always so embarrassing for her?

I slept with Alex.

Or, maybe: *The funniest thing happened last night... Alex and I accidentally...*

No, that wasn't the right way to start a conversation either.

"Emma?"

Startled, Emma glanced at Katie across the office desk. Her sister had wandered in about five minutes ago, wanting to talk about Knaresborough in central England.

"You okay?" asked Katie.

"Fine." Emma should spit it out, get it over

with so she wouldn't feel as if there was this huge secret between them.

"Did you hear what I said?"

"Sure," Emma replied. "The bed-and-breakfast in Knaresborough."

"Right," said Katie. "It's over two hundred years old now, and David was saying…"

Emma had never kept a secret from Katie before. Not that this was a secret, exactly. But she'd sure never slept with a man and not told her sister about it the next morning.

"…because with the new competition," Katie continued. "The probable payback on the redecorating costs would be fifty years."

Emma blinked.

"Does fifty years make sense to you?"

"Uh, not really. Katie, there's something—"

Katie stood up, a beaming smile on her face. "I totally agree. I'll tell David."

David? Wait. No. Emma wanted to talk about Alex.

"He can leave in the morning."

"Alex?"

Katie stared at her for a second. "David."

"For where?"

"Knaresborough, of course. What can he do from here?"

Right. The redecorating. "Okay. But, before you—"

Katie started for the door. "I'll get Legal to draft up an authorization for us to sign."

"Sure. But—"

"Can we talk later? He's going to be so excited."

"Katie—"

"Lunch?"

Emma sighed. "I can't. I promised Alex I'd stop by his place."

Katie waited, her hand on the doorknob.

"You know," said Emma, her stomach buzzing at the very thought of formal wedding plans. "Invitations, flowers, catering."

Katie's eyebrows waggled. "You have fun now, you hear?"

"Yeah. Right."

Have fun facing Alex after he'd seen her naked?

Have fun watching Philippe and Mrs. Nash reenact the Battle of Hastings?

Or have fun trying on a wedding gown while Amelia Garrison turned over in her grave?

None of it sounded particularly promising.

* * *

Amelia, it seemed, was a flapper, and maybe a bit of a rebel. Emma decided she liked that.

Her nineteen-twenties dress was made of gorgeous cream satin with a long, overlay bodice of ecru lace. Sleeveless, it had a cluster of ribbons at the shoulder and hip, and a flared skirt that shimmered to her ankles.

"You were right," she said to Mrs. Nash, turning in the wood-framed, oblong mirror in the Wiltshire bedroom, enjoying the whisper of satin against her skin.

"A perfect fit," Mrs. Nash agreed, brushing the skirt and arranging the scooped neckline. "And exactly right for a garden party wedding."

Emma paused. "Thank you for understanding about the church." Instead of an altar, she and Alex had decided on a rose arbor in the garden, overlooking the ocean.

"No point in lying to God along with everyone else."

It was a small consolation, but Emma was taking whatever she could get. "I said no to the proposal at first."

Mrs. Nash fussed with the ribbons at her shoulder. "But you said yes eventually."

"I did."

"And Alex got his own way again."

"Does he get his own way often?"

"He's a billionaire. He gets his own way pretty much whenever he wants to."

"But not with you?" Emma guessed.

Mrs. Nash gave her a sharp-eyed look. "Never with me."

"I bet he appreciates that. Somebody keeping him grounded, I mean."

"He hates it. So did his father. But his mother wouldn't let the man fire me."

Emma attempted to shift the conversation to the positive. "She obviously valued your help."

Mrs. Nash straightened. "No. She did it to spite him."

Emma honestly didn't know what to say to that.

"She was a misguided young woman, and he was a bitter old man."

"But, why—" Emma quickly cut off her inappropriate question.

"The money," said Mrs. Nash. "She wanted it.

He had it." Then Mrs. Nash shook her head. "She just didn't count on…the rest."

Emma tried to swallow the lump in her throat. She reminded herself that she had her own life, her own money, her own business. Alex wouldn't have any real power over her.

Mrs. Nash's voice turned brisk again. "I suspect she thought she'd outlive him."

Even though part of her dreaded the answer, Emma had to ask. "How did she die?"

"Horseback riding accident. Poor thing. Alex was only ten and a regular protégé for that cynical old bastard."

Emma shivered, struggling to find her voice. "Am I getting into bed with the devil?"

Mrs. Nash cocked her head, silent for a moment as she assessed Emma. "I'd say you'd already been to bed with the devil."

Emma was speechless. Did Mrs. Nash mean it literally? How could she possibly know?

Mrs. Nash gave an out-of-character chuckle as she went to work on the back buttons of the dress. "That's the trouble with the devil, young lady. He's irresistibly charming. Even to an old woman like me."

But Alex couldn't hurt Mrs. Nash. Where he could definitely hurt Emma. If she wasn't careful. If she didn't resist his charms on every possible level.

There was a sharp rap on the bedroom door.

"The invitations have arrived, ma'am."

"Thank you, Sarah," Mrs. Nash called. Then to Emma, "Philippe and Alex will be waiting downstairs."

Alex knew he had a problem as soon as he saw the expression on Emma's face.

"Six hundred and twenty-two?"

"You can add some more names if you'd like," said Mrs. Nash, her attention on one of the invitation samples. "We are *not* sending out scrollwork, script and purple fleur-de-lis under the Garrison family name." She gave Philippe a sharp look over the top of her glasses.

Emma waved the list at Alex. "Who are they? Your ex-lovers?"

The remark was uncalled for, and Alex clenched his jaw. "Hardly any of them."

Emma sniffed.

"The fleur-de-lis is a beautiful and honorable symbol," said Philippe. "It's an iris. For the goddess."

"I don't know six hundred people," said Emma. "I sure don't know three hundred."

Mrs. Nash squinted at the sample. "Good Lord, that butterfly hurts my eyes."

"You were thinking black and white?" asked Philippe.

"Silver," said Mrs. Nash.

"Blah," Philippe retorted.

"Maybe a little royal blue. Something dignified. Not this tacky, froufrou Technicolor explosion."

Alex couldn't care less what his invitations looked like. "Why are you making this into a thing?" he asked Emma.

She dropped her hand and the list into her lap. "I'm making six hundred and twenty-two things out of this."

"The garden is huge."

"That's not the point."

"What is the point?" He honestly wanted to know. What difference did it make if they got married in front of fifty guests or six hundred?

"Beef Wellington," Philippe suddenly sang out.

Emma turned to stare, while Mrs. Nash stilled.

"A compromise," said Philippe. "I will give up the fleur-de-lis if you agree to the *boeuf en croûte,* instead of your Yorkshire puddings."

"The Duke of Wellington's dish?" asked Mrs. Nash.

"Which he stole from Napoleon."

"After defeating him in the war."

Alex jumped in before the two could get going again. "Let's just say yes."

"And *I* have a compromise for you," said Emma.

Alex raised his brow.

"Your six hundred and twenty-two guests for a drive-through wedding in Vegas."

"Three hundred of them are yours," said Mrs. Nash, flipping her way through the invitation samples.

"What?" Emma's astonishment was clear.

"I spoke with your sister, and with your secretary."

Alex didn't even try to disguise his smug expression. "Three hundred of them are yours."

"Shoot me now," said Emma.

"Ahhh, mademoiselle," said Philippe, rising to put an arm around Emma. "It is no matter. You will be beautiful. The dinner will be magnificent. And people will forgive us for the insipid invitations."

"The flowers?" Alex quickly put in, before Mrs. Nash could make a remark that did justice to her expression.

Standing on the wide, concrete veranda, Emma watched a team of gardeners working on the expanse of lawn that stretched out to the cliffs at the edge of the Garrisons' property.

The tent would be set up on the north lawn. The arbor and guest chairs for the ceremony were slated for the rose garden. And a band would play in the gazebo. If the weather looked promising, a lighted dance floor would be constructed near the bottom of the veranda stairs.

The print shop would work overtime on the invitations tonight, and come next Saturday, she'd marry Alex. The guests likely had plans for that day. Heck, Emma already had plans for Saturday. But she'd cancel them and so would they. A garden wedding at the Garrison estate was too hot a ticket to miss.

Alex was counting on that.

And, as Mrs. Nash had said, being a billionaire, he usually got his way.

"Everything okay?" his voice rumbled behind her.

She coughed out a laugh. "What could possibly be wrong?"

He came up beside her. "Thought you might like to know they've agreed on the centerpieces."

"Yeah?"

"White roses and purple heather. Okay by you?"

The timbre of the lawn-mower motor changed, and she shrugged in response to Alex's question. "I really don't have an opinion on the centerpieces."

"You should."

"Why?"

"It's your party."

She pulled her gaze away from the two men in the rose garden to look up at him. "You feel at all funny about this?"

"Funny how?"

"Like a fraud?"

His eyes squinted down for a moment. "A little. I didn't expect to...."

"It's not like we're breaking the law," she said, more to herself than to him.

"We're throwing a great party, solidifying a business relationship, and giving the tabloids something good to write about for the next two weeks. I don't see the harm."

Emma didn't either, at least not from the logical perspective he'd outlined. But there was a problem at a visceral level.

"I guess I should ask you who pays for it," she said.

"Pays for what?"

"The party. The wedding. The six hundred guests. Are we splitting it down the middle?"

"I'll get this one," he said, crossing his arms to lean them on the rail, shifting his attention to the distant horizon. The ocean was growing restless, frothing up green and white as the tide rolled in. "You can catch the next one."

"The next wedding?"

"The next dinner."

"I doubt it'll be for six hundred."

Alex just shrugged.

"We need to talk about that," she said, matching his posture, leaning on the top rail and gazing out at the rhythmic waves.

"About dinner?"

"About how we're going to work this. Where are we going to live."

"Here. I thought we'd decided."

"*You* decided."

There was a smirk in his voice. "And your point?"

She elbowed him. "My point is, I get a vote, too."

"I'll pull a Philippe."

"How so?"

"A compromise. We stay here on weekends. Weekdays, we hang out in the city at one of the penthouses."

Emma had to admit that sounded reasonable.

"You do know we have to stay together?" he asked. "At least at first."

"I know. That solution sounds fine."

"Given any thought to the honeymoon?"

"Not even a moment." In fact, she'd been avoiding thinking about the honeymoon. This wasn't exactly any girl's dream scenario.

"What about Kayven Island?"

She twisted her head to look at him. "A McKinley resort?"

"Sure."

"I thought you'd fight tooth and nail for the *home court advantage.*"

"Will we be making any business deals on our honeymoon?"

"Wasn't on my agenda."

"Then you can have the home court advantage."

"It's not our best resort." Paris was bigger, and Whistler was most recently renovated.

Alex shrugged again. "I'd like to check out the island."

"A couple of days only—I'll book it. And I'm taking my laptop and PalmPilot."

"You afraid we'll get bored if we're alone together?"

A salt breeze gusted in off the ocean, and an image of Friday night when they were alone together bloomed in her mind. "Alex."

His expression said he was reading her mind.

"About Friday night…"

He waited.

"We can't do that again."

"Wanna bet?"

"Alex."

"I'm just saying we could if we wanted to."

"Well, we don't want to."

"You sure?"

"Yes! I'm sure. It was crazy and stupid."

"I thought it was exciting and satisfying."

She knew it was those things, too. But that didn't change the fact that it couldn't happen again.

"Just out of curiosity," said Alex. "What is your objection to it happening again?"

"This is a business deal."

"It's also a marriage."

She shook her head. What they were doing bore no resemblance whatsoever to a marriage. He was looking out for his interests, and she was looking out for hers. It was as simple as that.

"If we mix things up," she said. "If we get confused. One of us—and by one of us, I mean me—is going to get hurt."

Her hair lifted in the breeze, and he reached out to brush it back from her cheek. "I won't hurt you, Emma."

Despite the lightness of his touch, she knew it was a lie.

"Yes you will," she said. "Let's face it. You're

not marrying me because, of all the women in New York, I'm the one you want to spend time with." She gave a harsh laugh. "Heck, even when you narrowed the pool down to *McKinley* women in *New York City,* I came last."

"You did not."

"Alex. Don't rewrite history."

"I'm not—"

"At least do me the courtesy of being honest. You want my hotels. Well, you've got them. And that means you've got me for a while, too." She was falling for Alex. There was no point in denying it any longer. But the idea that Alex might also be falling for her was laughable. He could have any woman in New York City, probably any woman in the country. And he liked them glamorous, sophisticated and fashionable.

He was being kind right now, because deep down inside he really was a decent guy. And he seemed to like her. Sometimes, he seemed to like her a whole lot.

But she wouldn't delude herself. She wouldn't set herself up for heartache. They both knew he wasn't about to fall for plain old Emma McKinley just because he happened to be marrying her. Her chest burned as she forced herself to voice the bald truth. "But don't pretend it's anything other than a business deal."

He was silent for a full minute, his eyes dark as a storm-tossed sea, and just as unreadable.

"Fine," he finally said, a sharp edge to his voice. "I'll pay for the party. You live at my house. And we'll both bring our laptops on the honeymoon."

Then he turned from the rail and marched down the stairs.

Emma was glad. She'd said what needed to be said, and cleared the air between them. It was the only way to move forward.

Really.

Alex knew he had to back off. He was pushing Emma too hard and too fast. But he had a burning need to figure out what was going on between them. Truth was, at this moment, he had a feeling he'd pick Emma over anybody anytime anywhere. And that scared him.

From the moment they'd made love, he knew things had gone way past a business deal. They had something going on, and he needed to figure out what it was. To do that, he needed to talk to Emma. But she didn't want to talk to him. She especially didn't want to talk to him about them.

Them.

What a concept.

Alex stopped at the edge of the rose garden and gave his head a quick shake. His brain couldn't wrap itself around the idea of a them. He liked her. Sure. And he respected her, and she definitely turned him on. But what did that mean?

Did it mean he should give their marriage a chance? Or did it mean he was getting too caught up in the whole wedding charade?

He turned toward the balcony where she gazed out at the ocean, her hair lifting in the breeze. His heart gave a little hitch at the sight of her, and he knew one thing for sure. He wouldn't be getting any perspective at all while Emma was around.

Backing off was probably a good idea, for his sanity if nothing else. Besides, they'd ridden the publicity wave about as far as they could. From a business perspective, there was nothing left to do but get married.

And then they'd be together on the honeymoon, and maybe things would start to make sense. And, if it didn't, they'd have plenty of time to talk things out. After all, Emma had made it pretty plain they wouldn't be doing anything else.

Once Philippe and Mrs. Nash joined forces, the wedding plans shifted to high gear, barely leaving Emma time to take a breath. She stopped asking questions along about Wednesday, seeking sanctuary in her business problems instead. It was less stressful to worry about the proposed tourist tax regime in France than the music to which she'd say "I do."

Yesterday, Mrs. Nash had couriered a set of cardboard index cards, telling her where to go and what to do over the two days of festivities. Tonight the rehearsal dinner kicked things off. She and Katie were to dress at Alex's mansion in Oyster Bay. Then a limo would pick up the wedding party at seven. Alex's cousin Nathaniel would host a dinner for fifty at the Cavendish Club.

Afterward, the women would stay over at the mansion. Where, tomorrow morning, a veritable army of hairdressers, manicurists and makeup artists were due to arrive.

For the moment, Emma's stomach did a little flip-flop as her car rounded a curve and the mansion came into view. What the neatly typed index cards didn't cover was her reaction to Alex.

Katie popped forward in the passenger seat. "*This* is where you're going to live?"

"Only on weekends," said Emma, her voice firm with conviction. "And only for a few months."

Over the past week, she'd refocused her priorities. Her mind was on business now. Alex was simply a means to an end.

She wouldn't picture them together—not in his breakfast nook over a cup of coffee, not on his deck sharing a bottle of wine, and definitely not in his bedroom, in a tangle of sheets, his hot, naked body pressed up against hers.

"Can I come visit?" Katie asked, twisting her head as they passed the front rose garden.

Emma sucked in a bracing breath. "Sure," she said with determined cheer. Then Katie's phraseology penetrated. She'd said *I* not *we*. "What about David?"

Beneath her gauzy, mauve blouse, Katie

shrugged her shoulders. Her lips pursed every so slightly. "He's been working a lot of hours lately."

David's job interfering with his personal life?

"He works for you," Emma pointed out.

Katie tossed her head and let out a chopped laugh. "Never mind. It's nothing. Sometimes he hangs out with the guys at the club."

Emma pulled to a stop in the round driveway, turning to peer at her sister. "Is everything okay?"

Katie stared straight back. "Everything is great." She gestured to the wide staircase and the towering stone pillars. "Everything is fantastic! The Cavendish Club tonight, and the wedding of the year tomorrow. Now get your luggage and let's move in."

Emma nodded sharply in agreement. She could do this. She was ready for this.

Her cell phone buzzed, as two of Alex's staff members trotted down the stairs. She flipped it open and saw the Paris area code. Business before marriage. As it should be.

Nine

Alex stood at the bottom of the mansion's main staircase and listened to the hustle and bustle of the preparations. Mrs. Nash was taking a strip off a delivery man. Philippe was fussing over the temperature of the butter cream icing. And Katie was running around in a robe, worried about rose petals in the bathwater.

Only Emma seemed calm, serene really as she went along the hallway past Hamilton's portrait.

They were getting married tomorrow—in less than twenty-four hours—and she was talking to somebody in Paris, making sure the McKinley Inns convention display had arrived on time. She laughed at something the caller said, and her smile lit up the room.

He tried to remember the last time his house had felt like this. Maybe when he was a boy. Maybe when his mother was still alive.

His father had hated parties, but his mother had planned them anyway, sometimes for upward of a hundred. Alex could remember their arguments, and the way his father's jaw had tensed when the first guests arrived.

His gaze strayed to the landing at the top of the main staircase. As a young boy, he'd crept out of his room and peeked through the railing, watching finely coiffed women and snappily dressed men stroll through the foyer, drinks in hand, voices animated.

His mother had been happy on those nights. And the house had felt warm and alive. Like it felt now—with a woman present.

A certain glow worked its way up from the pit of his belly when he thought about Emma staying for a while. She looked up from her call and smiled at him before saying something in French into the phone.

Emma spoke French. And she seemed pretty much unflappable in the face of chaos.

Maybe they'd entertain some more. No harm in making the most of their time together. And fine parties with key contacts would do nothing but help their businesses thrive.

His own cell phone buzzed in his breast pocket, and he retrieved it, flipping it open.

"Garrison here," he said.

"It's your best man."

"Hey, Nathaniel. Where are you?"

"Just touching down in your backyard."

"You better not be blowing my tent over."

Nathaniel chuckled. "Relax. We're on the other side of the garage. You know you've got news crews circling, right?"

"They can circle all they want. We're going to the Cavendish Club tonight."

"Exactly. Still, I'm glad I'm not trying to get in your driveway."

"Did you happen to see a white cube van back there?"

"It's stuck behind a couple of semis and about a dozen limos."

"Good God. That's Philippe's tenderloin. I gotta get somebody out there to direct traffic."

"See you in a minute," said Nathaniel, signing off.

"Mrs. Nash," Alex called.

Emma plugged one ear and moved into an alcove.

Alex strode down the hallway and nearly ran into Katie.

"Can you please help me get her into the bath?" Katie pleaded.

"She's on the phone. Have you seen Mrs. Nash?" He continued toward the kitchen.

Katie scurried behind him. "I know she's on the phone. That's the problem."

"Well, I can't get her off. I have to rescue—"

The kitchen was a maelstrom of activity. That was the only way to describe it. A dozen cooks vied for space on the countertops. Two more were working over the stove. A cleanup crew was elbows deep in the sinks. And Mrs. Nash's voice rose clearly above the din as she spoke to a young man with a perpetually bobbing head.

"One *hundred* tables," she said. "The order was for white cloths with the royal blue skirting.

And I don't want a single wrinkle. If you can't guarantee—"

"Never mind," Alex muttered to himself, doing an about-face.

"*Alex,*" said Katie. "The hairdresser will be here in less than an hour."

Alex shook his head as he paced back down the hallway.

In the foyer, he picked the phone out of Emma's hand.

"Hey!"

"You, in the tub, now," he ordered, snapping it shut.

"*Alex,*" she protested, grabbing for the phone.

"Save it. I've got four hundred pounds of tenderloin to rescue." He swung open the big oak door.

"Hey, cousin," sang Nathaniel.

"Point me to the cube van."

Nathaniel ignored him and elbowed his way in. "This must be Emma," he cooed, taking Katie by both hands.

"I'm Katie," she corrected, tugging her hands away and closing the neckline of her robe.

"*Ahhh,*" said Nathaniel, hitting Alex with a sidelong look.

"What ahhh?" asked Katie, eyes narrowing.

"I'm Emma," said Emma, stepping forward to hold out her hand. "Alex has told me nothing but good things about you."

Nathaniel took Emma's hand with great fanfare and bestowed a kiss on her knuckles. "You're more beautiful than I imagined. And a most charming liar."

"What ahhh?" Katie repeated.

Nathaniel gave her a sharp look. "Wait your turn."

"*Excuse* me?" she said.

Nathaniel ignored her, clinging to Emma's hand.

"Would you do something for me?" Emma asked him sweetly.

"For you, anything."

"Make Alex give me back my phone."

Alex grasped her shoulders, turning her toward the staircase. "Bath."

Then he turned to his cousin. "And *you,* keep your hands off my bride."

"She's stunning," said Nathaniel with an exaggerated sigh, then he deigned to gaze down at Katie.

Katie stared back with a clenched jaw.

"Ahhh means I've heard about you, too," he said.

She was about to ask what he'd heard. Alex could see it in her eyes. But, to her credit, and to what had to be Nathaniel's disappointment, she didn't take the bait. She kept completely silent.

Head held high, she turned to link arms with Emma, and the women headed up the stairs.

"You're losing your touch, cousin," said Alex.

Nathaniel straightened his tie. "We already know she has terrible taste in men."

Alex slapped him on the back. "You cling to that thought. And help me get the damn tenderloin into the house."

After the wedding rehearsal and the dinner at Cavendish, Alex leaned on the railing of his veranda. It was after midnight, and the mansion was mostly dark. But the yard lights were on, and a few clouds teased a faraway moon.

"Not too late to back out," said Nathaniel, approaching with a crystal tumbler of single malt in each hand.

"I'm not backing out," said Alex. Worst case scenario, he'd make millions of dollars. Best case… He accepted the drink from Nathaniel and took a long swallow.

Best case, Emma decided to give them a real chance.

He'd given it a lot of thought over the past week, and there was something going on between them. It went past business, even past friendship, and he intended to use the honeymoon to figure out exactly what it was.

"The sister's prettier," said Nathaniel.

Alex straightened and shot his cousin a warning glare. "Excuse me?"

Nathaniel chuckled low.

"Emma happens to be gorgeous."

"Do you happen to be falling for your bride?"

"I'm simply pointing out the obvious."

"That she's gorgeous?"

"She is." Anyone could see that.

"And Katie's a pale second?"

Alex took another swig.

Had he once called Katie the pretty one?

Because Katie couldn't hold a candle to Emma. Emma was one of those rare women who got prettier as you got to know her. She had a stunning smile, eyes that glowed when she was happy and sparkled when she laughed. She had an inner radiance that nobody could fake.

"Katie's a pale second," he agreed.

Nathaniel sobered, and his jaw went tight. "You do remember she has an ulterior motive, right?"

"Katie?"

"Emma."

"I'm fully aware of all Emma's motives." She was doing exactly what she'd promised. The woman didn't have a scheming bone in her body.

"Al—"

"Back off, Nate."

"I'm just saying."

"Well stop saying it. My wife is not plotting against us."

"Everybody's plotting against us."

"You're paranoid."

"She's marrying you for your money."

"Because I forced her to."

"Just keep your guard up."

"Just mind your own damn business."

Nathaniel shook his head. Then his mouth curved into a knowing smile.

"What?" Alex asked.

"It's ironic," said Nathaniel.

Alex waited.

"That you fell for her."

"I did not." Alex snapped his jaw shut.

Okay. No point in disagreeing. He had fallen for Emma. But it hadn't clouded his judgment. For the first time in his life, his judgment was clear.

He was marrying Emma in the morning, and it was absolutely the right thing to do.

Emma told herself over and over that this wasn't a real wedding. But somehow it didn't ease the pain of her father's absence. Marriage of convenience or not, he should have been here to hold her hand, to escort her down the aisle, to tell her everything was going to be all right when, deep down in her soul, Emma feared it would never be all right again.

The weather had cooperated. So, under the glare of a brilliant blue sky, the gazebo band struck up the traditional version of the

"Wedding March." Mrs. Nash's choice, no doubt.

That was Katie's cue to start down the long strip of royal blue carpet that bisected seven hundred white folding chairs filled with smiling friends, relatives and business associates. Lilac ribbons streamed from the floral pew ends, fluttering in the breeze while Emma kept her attention fixed on Katie's purple dress.

Proving Alex lived in a whole other world, Mrs. Nash had hired a team of seamstresses to design and sew Katie's dress in less than a week. The same nineteen-twenties style as Emma's, it was shorter and simpler, and perfectly suited to Katie's slender shape.

They'd both opted for upswept hairstyles. To match the color of her dress, Katie's had a light sprinkling of irises at the back, while Emma had had a pinned French twist and the antique diamond tiara to match her cream-colored vintage gown. A veil seemed excessive, so she'd left her head bare.

Katie passed the midpoint of the long aisle, Emma's cue to start walking. She took a deep breath and pasted a smile on her face. She couldn't bring herself to meet anyone's eyes, and she sure didn't want to look at Alex, so she fixed her gaze on the rose-covered arbor.

Everything else faded to her soft vision, and she told herself her father would be proud. At least, she hoped he would be proud. She'd give anything to have him here to tell her one way or the other.

By the time she made it to the front, her eyes were misty with memories and regrets. Striking in his tux, Alex took her hands in his and stared at her quizzically while the preacher welcomed the congregation.

His eyes narrowed in a question, and she shook her head and forced a smile. She was fine. She would get this over with, and her life would get back to normal. Well, almost normal.

He gave her a smile in return and a reassuring little squeeze. Then the preacher addressed the two of them, talking at length on the solemnity of marriage and their obligations to each other as lifelong partners.

Emma grew more uncomfortable by the second. Was Alex listening to this? Had he known it was coming? Could they not cut to the "I dos" and get out?

Finally, the preacher started on the vows. Emma almost breathed a sigh of relief. But then her gaze caught Alex's, and his deep voice seemed to penetrate her very skin. She felt a tingle envelope her as he promised to love her and honor her.

It wasn't real. She'd repeated that to herself over and over again. But when she whispered her own vows, something shifted inside her. And when he slipped the antique wedding band on her finger, she felt the weight of a dozen generations on her shoulders. For better or worse, she was now a Garrison bride.

The preacher pronounced them husband and wife, the crowd erupted in a spontaneous cheer, and Alex leaned down to kiss her.

"For the record," he whispered as his palms cupped her face and lips grew close. "I *did* marry the pretty one."

Then his tender kiss exploded between them. He pulled back, far too soon. For a moment, and only for a moment, with her head tucked into the crook of his neck, inhaling his scent, feeling the strength of his arms and the power of his heartbeat, she let herself believe. But then she heard the helicopters in the distance and realized it was all for the benefit of the telephoto lenses.

Alex was grinning happily at her. He planted one more kiss on her forehead before taking her hand for the recessional. The band struck up, and the standing crowd congratulated them all the way down the aisle.

Back on the veranda, Katie gave her a quick hug and kiss, then they assembled into a receiving line to greet ambassadors, celebrities and captains of industry.

"You did great," said Alex nearly two hours later as they made their way across the lawn. The sky had turned a glorious pink. The champagne was flowing, and succulent smells were beginning to waft from the tent.

"I want to jump up on the nearest table and confess to them all," said Emma. The deeper they went into their deception, the guiltier she felt.

"I wouldn't recommend that," said Alex.

"Afraid I'd tarnish the Garrison name?"

He smirked. "Afraid you'd convince six hundred people you were a lunatic. I'd be forced to tell them you were merely drunk. It could get ugly."

"I didn't drink a thing."

"You mean I'd be, gasp, *lying?*"

"Don't you feel the least bit guilty?"

"At the moment, I feel…as if it's none of their damn business."

"You invited them to our wedding."

"To eat Beef Wellington, not to pass judgment on my life."

"They're your friends and family."

"You're my family now."

His words made her chest ache. "Don't say that."

In response, he took her hand and kissed each of the knuckles.

"Alex, don't." His playacting made her want things she couldn't have, things they could never have together.

"Emma. It's you and me now. And we'll make whatever damn decisions we want."

If only. But they weren't living in a vacuum. "What about Katie? And Ryan? And Nathaniel."

He sighed. "Are you always going to be this contrary?"

"My contrariness is a surprise to you?"

Before he could answer, Mrs. Nash bustled from the crowd, and he muttered in Emma's ear. "Knew I should have put obey in the vows."

"*There* you are." Mrs. Nash swiftly plucked some imaginary lint from the bodice of Emma's dress. Then she straightened Alex's tie. "They need you two at the head table."

"Nathaniel's written a great toast," said Alex.

Emma's stomach sank. She didn't think she could take any more benevolent smiles and heartfelt well wishes. "Surely you told him the truth."

"I haven't told him a thing."

"So his toast will be sincere?"

"He's going to call me lucky, and you gracious and beautiful."

The words, "I *did* marry the pretty one," suddenly rushed back into Emma's brain. What could Alex have meant by that?

Katie was stunningly gorgeous tonight. Even though she was on David's arm, half the men in the yard were staring openly at her, including Nathaniel, who looked annoyed about something.

"You *are* beautiful," Alex continued in a gentle voice. "And I *am* lucky. Focus on the truth, Emma."

It wasn't as simple as that. "Yet all those so-called truths are couched in one very big lie."

Had Nathaniel guessed what they'd done? Was that the reason for the scowl on his face?

"The head table," prompted Mrs. Nash.

"You have a half-empty attitude," Alex said to Emma.

"And you have flexible ethics."

"Emma, Emma." He put his hands on her shoulders, slowly guiding her toward the giant open-air tent. "Don't fail me now."

The speeches were over. The cake was cut. The Beef Wellington had been magnificent. And Emma was still holding up.

As the conductor cued up the first waltz, Alex counted his blessings and pulled her into his arms.

"Home stretch," he whispered, as much to have an excuse to lean in close as to reassure her. She knew her only remaining duty was to throw the bouquet.

To his delight, she almost immediately softened against him, matching his step to "Color My World." He'd chosen it because it was short. But it also seemed appropriate. He might not be in love with Emma, but she'd brought more life to his cavernous old house than he'd seen in years. He couldn't help but think his father would gripe about the noise. He also knew his mother would be pleased.

Vaguely aware of the oohs and ahhs of the crowd around them, he was infinitely more aware of the soft, sensual woman, pliant in his arms. Her guard was down, he imagined from exhaustion, but he wasn't going to dwell on the reason.

He planted a gentle kiss on the top of her head. Yeah, it would look good in the pictures. But, honestly, he felt like doing it. She'd been terrific today. In the receiving line, he'd been impressed with her graciousness all over again.

Maybe they could host some kind of Garrison-McKinley companies social function. Ryan would certainly be thrilled with the personal touch.

"We staying here tonight?" Emma asked, fatigue evident in her voice.

He shook his head. "Chuck will fly us to the airport."

A genuine laugh left her lips. "A helicopter ride from your backyard to the roof to the airport?"

"That's right."

"Okay. I'm not going to complain about that."

"You're *not?*"

She shook her head against his chest. "Not tonight. You can go ahead and spoil me to death."

He couldn't help but smile. "You got it."

The song ended, and a new one started up immediately. Emma would be relieved to have Nathaniel and Katie join them on the dance floor.

Alex caught sight of David scowling in the crowd. It was mean-spirited, but he was glad Nathaniel was making the man think. Taking a cushy job at his girlfriend's company? That was just tacky.

Nathaniel danced up beside them. "May I?" He nodded to Emma.

Alex's arms automatically tightened around her. *No.* He didn't want to stop dancing with Emma. And he didn't want lady-killer Nathaniel holding her close.

He felt a sudden pang of empathy for David.

"Certainly," he said smoothly, smiling at his cousin and forcing his arms to release her.

Then he turned to Katie to complete the switch.

"Great party," she told him, doing a hop step to catch up to his rhythm.

"Thanks."

"Think you'd be willing to host your sister-in-law's wedding?"

"My who?"

She tipped her chin to look up at him. "Me, of course."

"Oh."

"Think about it?"

"Sure."

They danced a few more steps. "So what's the story with your British cousin?"

"What do you mean?"

"He's very nosy."

"Is he asking about Emma?"

Was Nathaniel yanking his chain? Or did he still think Emma was a threat? And why was her smile so bright?

"Is that jealousy?" teased Katie.

"Don't be ridiculous." Alex dragged his attention away from Emma.

Nathaniel wouldn't flirt with his bride. Or would he? Had he come up with some bizarre plan to prove she was opportunistic?

He glanced at them again.

"You're as bad as she is," said Katie, digging her elbow into his ribs.

"Huh?"

"You can't keep your hands off each other."

Alex's jaw dropped. "Excuse me?"

"You heard me."

Had Emma actually told her they'd made love?

Katie waved a hand. "Give it up, Alex. You're not fooling anybody."

His heart thudded heavily in his chest. Katie knew they'd made love. Had she guessed how he felt?

He didn't even know how he felt.

He had to throw her off track. He carefully arranged his features and shrugged, feigning unconcern. "You know the score." He waited. "That thing on the cruise ship was…you know, just a thing."

Katie drew back, confusion on her face. "What thing on the cruise ship?"

Alex cursed himself and scrambled for a recovery. "We…had a fight."

"You two have fights all the time. One more would definitely not be memorable." Katie peered suspiciously into his eyes. "What happened on the cruise ship?"

"Nothing."

He knew the exact second comprehension hit her. "Oh my God."

"It's not—"

"And she didn't *tell* me? I'm going to kill her."

"No!" His arms reflexively tightened around Katie. "Don't you say a word."

"Why didn't she tell me? Why wouldn't she tell me?"

Alex could have kicked himself. "Back off, Katie. She's had a tough day."

"There's only one reason she wouldn't tell me," Katie muttered to herself, her feet tangling over the dance steps so that Alex had to recover for both of them.

"Because she regrets it," he said. She was afraid he would hurt her. And he might still. But then she might hurt him right back.

It was a chance they'd both have to take. They needed to work it out together. And alone.

Katie was shaking her head. "No, that can't be the reason."

He steered Katie toward Emma and Nathaniel.

She resisted his pressure. "Oh no you don't. You're not dumping me with him again."

Alex sure as hell was. "He's your official escort."

"He's my inquisitor."

"Katie?"

"Yeah?"

"Don't say anything to Emma about the cruise. It was a mistake. We both made a mistake."

Katie opened her mouth. But then she closed it again and nodded.

"Nate," said Alex.

Nathaniel glanced up and gave him a cocky, knowing grin. "Need your girl back?"

"I'm sure she's had enough of you."

"Why don't we ask her?"

But Alex latched on to Emma's arm, forcing Nathaniel to let go of her.

"Ahhh," said Nathaniel, staring down at his

returning partner. "The charming Katie. Where were we?"

"Let me save you some time," she said, adjusting her arm to keep a careful distance from him. "No. None of your business. And when hell freezes over."

Despite her efforts, Nathaniel dragged her closer, his voice fading as they spun away. "You know, you really shouldn't make promises you can't keep."

Emma blinked up at Alex. "What was that all about?"

"I don't think Nathaniel likes David."

She moved into step with him. "Well, neither do you."

Alex grunted. "That's because he's hiding behind Katie's skirts."

Emma punctuated her opinion with an exasperated sigh. "He's got an MBA. And he's a respected project manager."

"Then why's he hiding behind Katie's skirts? Why not make something of himself?"

"I'm way too tired to have this fight."

Alex felt like a heel. "Sorry."

"Hey, will you look at that."

"At what?"

Emma nodded across the floor. "Philippe is dancing with Mrs. Nash."

Alex followed the direction of her nod. Sure enough. And they were laughing about something.

"I guess they finally found some common ground," he said.

"That's good to see." Emma settled back in. "So what time is our flight to Kayven?"

"Whenever we want to go."

"You haven't booked the tickets yet?"

Alex smiled as he shook his head. "We don't need tickets. I have a plane."

Her shoulders relaxed, and she closed her eyes. "Naturally you have a plane." Then she rested her cheek against his chest, just the way he liked it. "And I'm not going to complain about that one either."

He rubbed his hand up and down her back. "I have to say, I really like your attitude."

"Don't get too used to it. All I need is a good night's sleep."

Ten

Alex was a perfect gentleman all the way to Kayven Island.

They'd stopped in L.A. for a late dinner. After which, Emma had had a surprisingly restful sleep across the Pacific, arriving at the local Kayven airstrip in the early morning hours.

Partway between Hawaii and Fiji, the island boasted white sand beaches, world-class reefs and turquoise seas dotted with brightly colored sailboats. The McKinley Resort consisted of a main building with traditional hotel rooms, an open-air lounge and a restaurant, along with several dozen bungalows scattered between towering palm trees.

Emma and Alex's bungalow opened onto a wide, covered patio with three steps down to the beach.

They quickly discovered their PalmPilots didn't work. Neither did their cell phones. Internet service was only available in the main building, and it was intermittent at best.

So, after an open-air breakfast of pastries and tropical fruit, Alex declared they should chuck their business obligations and rent a catamaran for the day. Inspired by the salt breeze and laid-back atmosphere of the island, Emma wasn't inclined to argue.

So, at 10:00 a.m., along about the time she usually attended her senior staff meeting, she was dressed in a lilac bikini, skimming over the waves of the South Pacific, the breeze in her hair and the salt spray dampening her skin.

"Dolphins," Alex called from the stern, and she twisted on the pontoon seat to see a dozen dorsal fins cutting through the green water.

"How do you know they're not sharks?" For the first time since leaving the dock, Emma cast a suspicious glance at the clear water below her.

Alex pulled the tiller. "Let's take a closer look."

"No!" she squealed. What did Alex know about sharks and dolphins? He'd spent his entire life in a city center just like her.

He laughed. "Chicken."

"I like my legs, thank you very much."

"They're dolphins."

"No offense, but you're hardly an expert."

He corrected their course to follow the towering cliffs of the shoreline. After a set of rudimentary instructions on sailing the two person catamaran, the man at the rental shop had provided a map to a snorkeling beach and one of the islands scenic coral reefs.

"I've watched the Discovery Channel," said Alex, his tone tinged with mock offense.

"I rest my case."

"You've got to learn to trust me on something."

"I'm letting you drive, aren't I?"

"*Letting* me?"

She whooped as they crested a particularly big wave, then sang out, "My turn on the way back."

"I don't think so."

"Hey, Alex. You've got to learn to trust me on something."

"You can decorate the main floor."

"The main floor of what?"

"Of my house."

She turned to stare at him. "We're decorating your house."

He stared out over the waves, and she had to fight to keep from ogling his wet, tanned body. His calves were sculpted with muscle, and his pecs were something out of a beach-boy magazine. His face was handsome as ever, but the rakish swirl of his windblown hair left him looking softer, less intimidating than he had in New York.

She was suddenly aware that they'd be spending the day on a deserted beach, far away from the problems and constraints of their real lives. She'd sworn up and down, to herself and to Alex, that they were never, ever making love again. Now she found herself questioning that promise, exploring the rationale and trying to remember exactly why it was so important that she keep her hands off him.

"I thought we'd decorate before the party," he said.

She shook herself out of the fantasy. "Huh?" *What party?*

"I thought a Garrison-McKinley company

party might be a nice idea. Ryan is always after me to soften my image."

She gave her head a shake. "You want another party? After yesterday? Or was it the day before?"

"Actually, I think this might be our wedding day."

"Don't mess with me."

"I'm not messing with you. The International Date Line takes a funny jog around Kiribati."

She refused to be impressed by his knowledge. "Well, it's only noon," she retorted. "That means we're not married yet."

He squinted. "Hmmm. That means there's time for one last fling."

Emma made a show of glancing around the empty ocean. "With who?"

Alex waggled his eyebrows.

"In your dreams." Or in her dreams, depending on how you looked at it.

"Look," he said. "There's the point and the bent palm tree." He abruptly turned the tiller, sending the blue-and-red sail swinging cross-ways over the catamaran.

Emma shaded her eyes as a sparkling white,

crescent-shaped beach came into view. Cliffs towered over it on both sides, and a white, frothy waterfall spilled into the little cove.

"Wow." She let out a long breath of appreciation. "I don't think we're in Manhattan anymore."

"Screw the cell phones," said Alex. "The world can live without us for a day."

Emma laughed and shook off the remaining vestiges of her guilt, while the sail caught a gust of wind, pushing the front of the floats onto the soft sand.

She quickly hopped off the net platform, sinking calf-deep in the warm water, and grabbing the rope as the floats bobbed free again.

Alex joined her and tugged the boat onto the sand and removed their supply sack.

She pulled her messy hair free of the elastic and raked it into a new ponytail. Without the breeze from the moving sailboat, the sun was burning hot. And the water was more than inviting.

"Swim first or snorkel?" asked Alex, reading her thoughts.

"Anything that gets me wet."

They swam in the cove and snorkeled around

the reef for hours. With the swim fins for propulsion, Emma easily maneuvered through the salt water, seeing thousands of fish in every color imaginable, crabs, sea urchins and sea stars, plants and shells, and what seemed like mile upon mile of vibrant coral.

Thirst and hunger finally brought them to the surface. The sun had moved far enough in the sky that they could find shade from one of the cliffs. They spread their blanket out near the waterfall, where the fine spray brought the air temperature down a few degrees.

Emma leaned back and inhaled the scent of the tropical flowers, then she closed her eyes to concentrate on the calls of birds and the low hum of the insects. A sigh slipped out. "Do we really have to go back?"

Alex's sexy voice was full of promise. "No, we don't."

She opened one eye, squinting at him through her sunglasses as he lay down on the blanket, propping himself up on one elbow.

She matched his pose so that she was facing him. "Eventually, we'd starve."

He pushed his sunglasses up on his forehead,

shifting almost imperceptibly forward. "We'd survive on fish and coconuts."

"You're going to fish."

"I'm a versatile guy."

"How are you going to cook them?"

He moved her sunglasses up on her forehead. "I'll gather firewood from the forest."

The mere whisper of his touch spiked her pulse. "And rub two sticks together?"

"If I have to. I didn't become a billionaire by giving up."

"I thought you became a billionaire by inheriting lots of money."

He moved closer. "Yeah. There was that. But it doesn't mean I'm not a resourceful guy." His gaze dipped to her cleavage, and a buzz of sexual awareness ran through her.

"Alex."

"It's okay." He reached for the spaghetti strap on her bikini top, running his index finger beneath it, then trailing it down her arm. The fabric peeled away, exposing the barest millimeter of her nipple.

His eyes darkened, and she could feel the sensuality radiating from his very pores. Next, he leaned forward and kissed the tip of her shoulder, his cool lips gentle on her sun-warmed skin.

She knew she should fight it, but the last thing in the world she wanted to do was interrupt a sexy man on a tropical beach, making her feel like she was the most desirable woman in the world.

He left her shoulder to kiss the mound of her breast, trailing his fingertips along the curve of her waist.

She gasped in a breath, and his arm went solidly around her, turning her onto her back, his dark head blocking out the bright sunshine.

"I want you," he said.

And she wanted him, too. So much that it hurt to breathe. Her chest was tight. Her skin was tingling. And her thigh muscles pulsated with the need for his touch.

"Oh, Alex."

He bent his head close to hers, kissing the corner of her mouth.

"It's okay," he muttered. "It's after three. We're married now."

Before she could smile, he kissed her full on the lips, his broad hand swooping beneath her bottom to pull her against him.

She opened her mouth, tangling with his tongue. And her hands framed his face, pulling herself closer and deeper, trying desperately to fuse her body to his.

The waterfall roared in her ears, and the breeze off the ocean sensitized her skin. She kissed his cheek, his shoulder, the bulge of his bicep, tasting the sea salt, reveling in the flavor of his arousal.

He flicked the clasp of her bikini top, and the purple fabric fell away, exposing her breasts to the heat of the sun and Alex's avid gaze.

"The pretty one," he muttered. "The beautiful, sexy, charming sister. I am so glad you stormed into my office that day."

Emma tried to comprehend his meaning, but the words didn't make sense. And then he drew her nipple into his mouth, and the entire world stopped making sense. It was Alex. And they were married. And she was falling fast and hard and unconditionally for him.

The rake of his teeth and the swirl of his tongue sent pulses of delight streaking down her body. She arched her spine, tipping her head back, closing her eyes against the rainbow of light taking over her brain.

She had to feel him. She had to touch him. She had to make sure he was experiencing *half* the intensity she was.

She ran her hands up his arms, resisting the urge to linger, exploring his biceps and strong shoulders. Then she tangled her fingers in his hair, pulling him tight against her breast, releasing a pent-up moan of desire.

He moved to the other breast, and she trailed her fingertips down his back, shifting her knees and pressing his arousal into the cradle of her thighs.

He drew back. "Whoa. You sure?"

"Yes," she blurted. "I'm sure. I *want you*. Whatever. Just tell me what to say."

He chuckled as he kissed her mouth. "I meant are you sure you want it this fast."

"Yes. Now. Right now." She didn't think she could wait another second.

He sobered, his thumb hooking her bikini bottom and sliding it off over her sweat-slicked skin. Then he made short work of his own trunks, positioning himself over her, staring down at her with tousled hair and dark eyes, like some kind of sea god bent on conquest.

His fingertips trailed down the slight indentation of her belly, and she squirmed beneath him, holding her breath, waiting, anticipating. He stared deep into her eyes and smoothed over her curls, parting her thighs and easing his finger into her body.

She sucked in a breath with the exquisite pulse that came to life deep inside her. She slid her own hand down his body, cupping him, controlling him, pulling him toward her to satisfy her growing impatience.

He swore under his breath.

Then he pushed her hand away and flexed his hips, pressing himself at her entrance, widening her, stretching her, sliding slick and thick and hot inside her, inch after delicious inch as his hands tangled with hers and their mouths fused once more.

Primal passion took over.

The birds called in the treetops, the waterfall cooled the raging fever of their skin, and Alex's rhythm matched the pulsating waves taking over their gleaming stretch of beach.

He sped up, then slowed down, and she bit her lip, pushing back against his hands, arching her spine and tipping her hips to bring his thrusts faster and harder against her.

Then the world seemed to freeze. Her breathing stopped, and the sun disappeared, the trees went silent and she cried his name as the rainbow sensations washed over her again and again and again.

His own cry was guttural, and the parrots took flight above them, a cacophony of surprise and confusion. Then his weight finally settled, pressing her into the warm sand, his arms, his breath, his heartbeat surrounding her.

By the time they made it back to their bungalow, dusky pink clouds were gathering above the island.

Then, while the maître d' sat them in the resort's open-air restaurant, the first fat raindrops plunked on the palm leaves and turned the wooden deck a dark mottled brown. Lightning flashed in the distance, and the growing rainstorm clattered against the restaurant's thatched roof.

Grateful for the cool air, Emma settled back in

the cushioned teak chair, dangling her sandal from her toes while the cool breeze swirled around her cotton print dress. The hurricane lamps on the tables seemed to brighten as the orange ball of the sun disappeared below the horizon.

Emma gazed at the flickering light on Alex's handsome face, hardly believing they'd so thoroughly consummated their marriage.

"What are you thinking?" he asked.

She grinned. "That I'm married to the best-looking man in the room."

He glanced around. "Okay," he said slowly. "But the other guys are mostly over sixty."

A waiter in a pristine white jacket approached. "Mr. and Mrs. Garrison. I am Peter, the restaurant manager. The chef was delighted to hear you would be dining with us tonight. He has asked if he might present some additional entrée suggestions?"

Alex stood up and shook the waiter's hand. "Good to meet you, Peter. Please, tell the chef we would be delighted to hear his suggestions."

"Very good." With a smile and a nod, Peter retreated, only to be replaced by their cocktail waiter.

"Champagne?" Alex raised his eyebrows in Emma's direction.

"For our wedding night?" she asked with a stupid, sappy grin. But she couldn't help it. It was still Saturday and, if the expression in Alex's dark eyes was anything to go by, they were about to spend a glorious night together.

He nodded to Emma, then turned to the waiter. "Cristal Rose? The ninety-six?"

The waiter nodded sharply. "Excellent." Then he swiftly removed their red and white wine-glasses and left the table.

Alex reached for her hands and took a deep breath. "So, you want to talk about this? Or do we just let it happen?"

She let the warmth of his touch penetrate her skin. "The champagne?"

He shook his head, stroking his thumb over her rings. "No. Not the champagne."

"Let me see." She tilted her head. "The chef?"

"No. Not the chef."

"Your inability to steer a catamaran?"

"Hey."

"You nearly took out those two tourists."

"Their dive to the left was incredibly sudden."

"They were scattering in terror."

Alex paused, then he sobered. "May I assume your redirecting the conversation means you just want to let it happen?"

His words sent a shiver through her, and she leaned forward, lowering her voice. "I'm not even sure what 'it' is yet."

He gave her fingers a gentle squeeze. "I am," he said softly.

An unaccountable panic burst through her belly. "Don't—"

"I won't. Not tonight."

"Mr. and Mrs. Garrison," Peter interrupted. "May I present Chef Olivier."

Alex released Emma's hands, and she tucked her hair behind her ears as the wind picked up another notch.

Alex got to his feet. "A pleasure," he said to Chef Olivier, shaking the man's hand.

"The pleasure is mine," the chef replied.

"Are you cold?" Peter inquired of Emma. "Shall we close the shutters?"

"Please, don't," said Emma. There was something wildly beautiful about the pounding rain, the distant lightning, and the crazily undulating palm fronds. There was a potent storm brewing out on the Pacific, and a potent storm brewing inside her. Both were frightening, unpredictable and exhilarating all at the same time.

Eleven

"I want to say it," said Alex, propping himself up on one elbow in their huge four-poster bed.

"You can't say it," Emma responded, her sun kissed breasts glowing a golden honey against the stark white sheets.

"But I mean it," he insisted. He'd realized hours ago that he was madly, passionately, incredibly in love with his wife.

She reached up to place her index finger across his lips. "You promised."

He drew her fingertip into his mouth, turning the suction into a kiss. "Bet I can make you say it."

She shook her head in denial, but he knew that

he could. The right kiss, the right caress, the right whisper in her ear, and her secrets were his for the taking.

It wasn't ego. It simply was.

He feathered his fingers up the length of her thigh.

"Don't," she gasped.

He smiled. "Say it."

"Play fair."

"All's fair in—"

"*Alex.*"

He moved his hand and kissed the tip of her nose. "I'm just messin' with you."

"Well, I don't like it," she said tartly.

"Sure you do. At least give me that."

Her mouth twitched in a reluctant half smile.

The telephone next to the bed jangled in his ear. He swore out loud.

"What time is it?" she groaned, covering her ears in time for the second ring.

"Around one," he said, picking up the receiver before it could vibrate his eardrums a third time. "Yeah?"

"Where the *hell* were you?" barked Nathaniel.

"Dinner. The beach. Why?"

"Because you're about to lose half a billion dollars, that's why."

Alex sat up straight, his brain shifting gears faster than a Formula One driver. "What happened? Where are you?"

"David happened. And I'm still in New York."

"David?" asked Alex.

Emma sat bolt upright. "What about David? Is Katie all right?"

Alex held up a finger. He wasn't trying to be dismissive, but he needed to hear what Nathaniel had to say.

"*David,* that slimy, underhanded son-of-a-bitch, is attempting to *sell* the Kayven Island Resort."

Alex reflexively glanced around. "Huh?"

"Please, cousin, tell me you're a director of McKinley Inns. Tell me the paperwork is done. Tell me Emma and Katie don't still have control of that company."

Alex's gaze shifted to Emma.

"What?" she asked.

"Alex?" Nathaniel prompted.

"The lawyers are drafting right now."

"Are you telling me *nothing's* been signed?"

"Only the loan to McKinley."

"Shit."

Alex's tone was harsh. "What the hell is going on, Nate?"

"Cranston's flashing a power of attorney signed by those two women."

That didn't make any sense. None at all. "Hang on." Alex covered the receiver.

Emma was watching him with an impatient look of confusion.

He kept his voice even. It had to be a mistake, or maybe a forgery. "Nathaniel says David Cranston has a power of attorney."

She drew back on the bed, shifting the covers away. "For what?"

"Did you sign anything for him?"

She shook her head. "No." Then she stopped shaking and her eyes narrowed. "Wait. There was one thing. An authorization to redecorate a bed-and-breakfast in Knaresborough. It's a tiny little place. Nothing important."

Alex returned to the phone. "She says all he can do is redecorate some bed-and-breakfast."

"It's not redecorating. And it's not a bed-and-breakfast. The man is authorized to sell any and all McKinley properties. He's cutting a deal with Murdoch and DreamLodge. For an obscene commission."

"How do you know—don't answer that." Alex went back to Emma. "Did you read it carefully?"

Her eyes went wide, and her face paled.

"Did you read it at all?"

"We'd already talked about it…" Her features pinched, and her hands fisted around the blanket. "With the wedding and all… I signed so many stacks of paper."

He let out a pithy swearword.

"Yeah," said Nathaniel. "Now you're catching on. You get your ass on a plane."

Alex glanced to the rain battered window and the pitch black beyond. "Can you stall?"

"I've already put his entire legal team on retainer, had them declare a conflict of interest, and forced him to find new attorneys. You don't want to know what that cost me."

"Did you talk to Katie."

"Hell, yes."

"Can she stop it?"

"Not without Emma."

Alex closed his eyes and willed the wind

and rain to *stop.* "We'll be there as soon as humanly possible."

"Get here now." The line went dead.

Alex set down the phone.

"Alex?" Emma whispered hoarsely.

He stared at her. There was no easy way to say this. "David is trying to sell the Kayven Island Resort."

She blinked back in silence. "Why?"

Alex's stomach clenched to walnut size.

Why?

Because its value is about to rise to half a billion dollars.

Sorry I forgot to mention that before you married me.

Emma understood the words "trying to sell Kayven Island." It was the meaning that eluded her.

David was redecorating in Knaresborough. And, as far as she knew, hadn't had anything to do with the Kayven Island property.

"Why would he do that?" she repeated into the rain-dotted silence. She got that something was wrong. But she couldn't get the puzzle pieces to connect inside her head.

"For a big, fat commission from Murdoch." Alex raked a hand through his hair. "Why didn't Katie see—"

"Back up," said Emma, clambering off the bed and shrugging into one of the hotel robes. "Murdoch?"

Alex's eyes went hard as granite. "Murdoch bribed David to find a way to sell him Kayven Island."

"He wanted it that bad?" Sure it was a nice resort, but it served a small niche market. It commanded steep rates, so it was often half empty. Nobody was getting rich off Kayven Island anytime soon.

A muscle clenched near Alex's right eye. He grabbed his boxers and retrieved a pair of slacks from the closet. "We have to get to the airport."

"In *this?*"

"It'll let up eventually. As soon as there's a break in the ceiling, we're taking off."

"But what did Nathaniel say?"

Alex seemed completely serious about head-ing for the airport, so Emma discarded the robe and pulled on a cotton dress.

"Just what I told you," said Alex.

"You haven't told me anything."

Keeping his back to her, he moved around the room as he spoke. "David duped you and Katie into signing a power of attorney that somehow allowed him to make a deal on Kayven Island. Nathaniel is trying to hold him off, but we need to get back to New York."

Emma watched his furtive packing. "What aren't you telling me?" Was it a done deal? Had they already lost the resort?

"Nothing."

"Has the sale gone through?"

"No."

"Because if it has, it wouldn't be the end of the world."

Alex froze.

"It wouldn't," she repeated. "As long as David got a decent price."

Alex pivoted to face her. "Your employee, your sister's *boyfriend,* is trying to defraud your company and you're saying it'll be okay *as long as he got a decent price?*"

"If you're afraid to tell me it already happened, you—"

"I'm not afraid to tell you it already happened. It *didn't* already happen."

"Then why are you acting so weird?"

"I'm not acting weird. I'm acting normal. Acting weird was earlier."

His words hit Emma like a sledgehammer, and she staggered back. Was that it? Had the kinder, gentler Alex been an illusion? Was he mad now because he thought she'd made a mistake?

She supposed she had made a mistake. But Katie had—

Katie.

Katie would be devastated.

Emma went for the phone.

But as she reached for the receiver, Alex latched on to her wrist.

"What are you doing?"

"Calling Katie."

"You can't do that."

Emma glared up at him. "Yes, I can." This wasn't some random whim, this was her sister's life.

"Emma…"

"Let go of me, Alex."

"We have to talk."

She tried to shake him off. "We can talk on the plane."

"We have to talk *before* you talk to Katie."

The look in his eyes sent a shiver of fear through her body. She almost couldn't bring herself to say the words. "Is she hurt?"

"*No.* No. She's not hurt."

Emma shook her arm, and Alex let her go.

"Then what the hell is going on?" she asked.

Alex squeezed his eyes shut for a second. "There's something about Kayven Island you don't know."

"But Katie's not hurt?"

"Katie's fine. I think she's with Nathaniel. No, I know she's with Nathaniel. He won't let her out of his sight until we get back."

Emma's fear cranked back up. "Is she in some kind of danger?"

"Emma, listen to me."

She closed her mouth.

Alex took both her hands in his. "The local government is putting a cruise ship dock on the island."

"What island?"

"This island."

"So?"

"So, that's why Murdoch wants the resort. That's why he's willing to bribe David."

"Because the value will—" Emma stopped.

She got it. In a blinding flash she understood exactly what had happened to her.

"Alex!"

"I wanted it, too," he confessed.

No kidding. She yanked her hands from his, stumbling back against the bed.

"You kept this from me?"

"Yes."

"You… You… *I* could have sold it to Murdoch."

Alex nodded.

"And then I wouldn't have had to marry you."

He nodded again.

She raised her fist, battling a split second temptation to pummel his chest. "And you didn't *tell* me?"

"It was business."

"Business?"

"I knew what I knew, and I did what was best for my company."

The fight suddenly left her.

Of course he'd done what was best for his company. He'd never pretended to do anything different. He'd even warned her. He'd suggested she do the same.

And she thought she had, she thought she was. But Alex had been working against her all along.

"And you have the nerve to criticize *David?*" she challenged.

Alex gritted his teeth. "I am *nothing* like David. David's a con artist and a criminal."

"Yeah," Emma agreed. "Just look what he did? He romanced Kayven Island out from under Katie."

Emma had never felt like a bigger fool in her life. She might be stuck with Alex for better or worse, but that didn't mean she ever had to speak with the man again.

"And wasn't that reprehensible of *him?*" she ground out in a parting shot, then turned away and cut him out of her life forever.

Emma forcibly tamped down her troubles with Alex as soon as she saw Katie's stricken face.

They were in the McKinley offices. It was six in the evening. She wasn't even sure what day.

"Oh, honey," she crooned, drawing Katie into an embrace.

Alex and Nathaniel immediately put their heads together and began talking in low tones.

Katie hiccoughed out a sob. "I've made such a mess."

"It's not your fault." Emma shook her head, then shot Alex and Nathaniel a look to ensure they kept any stray opinions to themselves. "The only thing you're guilty of doing is trusting too much. We were coerced and lied to by criminals."

Katie swallowed. "I should have guessed—"

"Guessed what?" asked Emma, her gaze still boring in on Alex's profile. "That a man could make love to you one minute then stab you in the back the next?" Emma hadn't guessed that, either. But she'd know better next time.

Alex spared her a fleeting glance, his expression neutral. She wasn't even sure her words had registered. Not that her condemnation would mean a thing to him anyway.

"The important thing is to fix it," she said,

switching her attention to Katie, pulling back and striving for a look of reassurance.

Katie gave a shaky nod, her gaze darting nervously to Nathaniel, and Emma worried what the man might have said before they arrived.

"We have to both sign a revocation," said Katie. "The lawyers…"

Alex stepped forward. "The lawyers have it drafted, and they're waiting across the hall."

Emma refused to look at him. "And then what?" she asked Nathaniel.

Alex gave a frustrated sigh.

"Then we make certified copies and have a sheriff waiting to serve it to both Murdoch and Cranston first thing in the morning."

"And that's it?" asked Emma.

Nathaniel shrugged. "That's it."

She turned to Katie. "See? It's going to be fine."

Katie shook her head, mutely blinking back tears, and Emma felt like a heel.

"Hey, I know you'll miss him."

Katie's face crumpled, and Emma pulled her back into her arms. Then she motioned for Alex and Nathaniel to leave. The papers were ready. All it took was their signatures before the start of business tomorrow. She could afford to comfort Katie for a few minutes.

The door snapped shut behind the men.

"I'm such a fool," said Katie.

"You're not a fool."

Emma had made a much bigger mistake. And, while they could recover from Katie's, Emma's was permanent. Alex would soon own half of their business, and there wasn't a single thing they could do about it.

Katie pulled back, a funny expression coming over her face. "If it wasn't for Nathaniel, we'd have lost millions."

"If it wasn't for me, we'd have made millions."

Katie shook her head. "That was just business."

"You're *defending* Alex?"

"He could have had our loan called and cut us out completely."

"Or he could have been *honest.*"

"He was honest. He gave us the choice between a hostile takeover or a merger. We took the merger."

A merger? That's all it was to Katie?

Then Emma forced herself to regroup.

Yes, that's all it was to Katie.

Katie didn't know about Kayven Island. She didn't know that Alex had tried to seal the deal by pretending to fall for her. She didn't know that he'd been willing to coerce some friendly sex out of his bride of convenience before they got down to the business of flipping her resort for half a billion bucks.

Alex Garrison in love with Emma McKinley.

If anyone had told her two months ago she'd have dared to even think that phrase, she'd have laughed them out of the room. But she'd not only thought it. For a moment in time, she'd believed it. On that faraway beach, she'd believed it with all her heart. And he heart was what she'd given to Alex. And her heart is what he'd crushed with his bare hands.

He'd wanted her hotel, and she'd been stupid enough to hand him that and more on a silver platter.

Katie looked aghast. "How will I ever trust my own judgment again?"

It was Emma's judgment that needed remedial attention.

"I asked..." Katie tapped her fingertips

against her mouth. "I asked Alex if he'd host our wedding someday." Then she have a helpless laugh. "What a fool I was."

"Katie, please—"

The office door opened. "Emma," said Alex. "We have to do this."

Emma looked at Katie. "You ready?"

She gave a shaky nod. "Yeah."

By 8:30 a.m., ten cups of coffee to the good, Alex was ready to jump out of his skin waiting for the sheriff to show.

"Screw it," he growled to Ryan who was sitting across the boardroom table, tapping a pen against the polished, inlay pattern.

Ryan's brow jerked into a furrow. "Screw what?"

Alex slid the manila envelope into his palm. "I'm delivering them myself."

Ryan stood up, pushing the chair back behind him. "Whoa there, Alex. I don't think that's such a good idea."

"Why not?" He couldn't stand sitting there another second. And at least he'd know it was done right.

"Because we don't want to have to waste our lawyer's time clearing you of assault charges."

"David won't even be there."

"Murdoch will."

"Murdoch's too old to defend himself."

"My point, exactly."

Alex snorted as he stood. "Right. Like I'm going to assault an old man." But he did want to see Murdoch's face when they presented the documents that would undo what he'd done.

The negotiations had moved far enough, with David legally entitled to conduct them, that backing out now could get dicey. Their lawyers had advised the most expedient way out was for Alex's company to present an outrageous counteroffer so that Murdoch would be forced to withdraw. Quick and neat, and Alex was at the helm. First things first though, they had to deal with that proxy.

"It's not like there's anything to negotiate with him," said Ryan. "You don't even have to have a conversation."

"I just want to see his face." Alex was still doing a slow burn. "I told him *I* was the contact. He ignored me. That makes it personal."

"You sure it's not Emma that makes it personal?"

Alex slid a glance Ryan's way.

"How was the honeymoon?" Ryan asked mildly.

"Short," said Alex.

"You didn't call in yesterday. Not once. Not to anyone."

Alex retrieved his briefcase and placed the envelope inside. "No cell service."

"No phones in the hotel."

"We were busy."

Ryan grinned. "It went well?"

Alex snapped the case shut. "I guess that's irrelevant now that she knows about Kayven."

Ryan sobered. "Yeah. I guess it is."

"Yeah," Alex agreed, trying very hard not to care.

Sure, Emma was upset. But she'd get over it. And he had what he wanted. He had what they'd all wanted: a ring on her finger and a fifty-percent share in McKinley Inns.

And... He scooped the briefcase from the table and headed for the door. He was about to rescue the jewel in the McKinley crown and visit revenge on an annoying rival.

"You okay?" Emma whispered, walking up behind Katie and stroking the back of her soft blond hair.

Her sister was sitting on the bench seat in the bay window of the penthouse dining room, staring at the wispy clouds on the eastern horizon. The coffeemaker dripped and hissed on the countertop.

Katie nodded. "What about you?" They'd sat up most of the night talking, so Katie knew all about Alex and the honeymoon.

Emma took the other end of the bench seat, curling her legs under her robe. "My stomach aches, but I think it's embarrassment more than anything else."

At least that's what she was telling herself.

She closed her eyes and sighed. Alex and Ryan and Nathaniel must all be having a good laugh at her expense. She'd fallen for his act hook, line and sinker.

"They must have been afraid I'd back out," she whispered, leaning one elbow on the white windowsill, supported the weight of her achy, sleep-deprived head.

Thinking about it, she realized her decreasing objections to the marriage correlated to when Alex started acting as though he liked her. He'd obviously figured out really quick that she was a desperate, lonely, plain-Jane woman, ripe to fall for pretty much anybody.

And he'd used that as a way to control her. Who knew if he even wanted sex with her. Maybe he just thought she wanted sex with him. And he was willing to play the gigolo, if it meant sealing the deal.

The pretty one. He'd actually hinted she was prettier than Katie. What's more, she'd actually started to believe him.

Alex had earned his millions through acting alone.

Katie squeezed her shoulder. "It's going to be okay." But her voice was too hollow to be convincing.

"I can't divorce him," said Emma. "I'd lose a fortune."

"Then we'll go away. We'll go on a very long vacation."

Emma nodded. She'd promised to live with Alex and hang on his arm like some kind of accessory. But that part wasn't in writing. So he'd just have to learn to live with the disappointment.

She only hoped she could learn to live with it. Despite her resistance, she'd started to like the life he'd made up. She'd even started looking forward to that goofy McKinley-Garrison office party. And redecorating his main floor. It would have been fun to redecorate his main floor. Even if it was only temporary.

A tear slipped out of the corner of her eye.

Who was she kidding?

She'd stopped thinking about it as temporary somewhere on the hot beach at Kayven Island, along about the time Alex pretended he loved her, and she realized she loved him right back.

She inhaled a shuddering sob.

Katie wrapped her in a tight embrace. "Oh, Emma. It's going to be okay."

But it wasn't going to be okay. It might never be okay again.

Twelve

Alex was going to make things right. And he was going to make Clive Murdoch regret the day he even considered crossing Alex Garrison.

He slapped the envelope down on Murdoch's desk.

"What's this?" the old man asked, glancing from the envelope to Alex.

"Our counteroffer."

Murdoch's eyes narrowed.

Alex plopped down in one of the guest chairs. "To bring you up to speed. David Cranston's authority to negotiate for McKinley's has been revoked."

Murdoch's face went from pasty to ruddy. "That's—"

"He's lucky he's not in jail. You're lucky—"

"He has a duly executed power of attorney."

"*Had.* I'm the man you have to deal with now."

Murdoch snatched up the envelope. "We'd already agreed on a price."

Alex nodded. "That you had. And I'm willing to stick to that price, provided you agree to the in-kind contribution McKinley's requesting."

Murdoch peeled away the envelope and stared at the first page of the contract. Then he stared bug-eyed over the page at Alex, and his ruddy complexion turned near purple.

For a second, Alex worried the man was going to have a heart attack.

"*Free* staffing?"

"For all McKinley properties, around the globe, into perpetuity."

"That's—"

"Perfectly legal, according to my, and your former, legal team. You are, of course, free to turn it down."

Murdoch opened his mouth, but nothing emerged except a damp squeaking sound. It took him a few seconds to recover the power of speech. "This is outrageous."

"This is business," said Alex, clamping his jaw. "I told you to deal with me and me alone. What's more, I told you *nothing* of McKinley's was for sale."

"Because you wanted it for yourself."

"That's true," said Alex. "And I got it." But things had changed.

Murdoch's mouth twisted in an ugly sneer. "I sure hope it was worth the mercy screw."

Alex was out of his chair in a flash, reaching across the desk and grabbing Murdoch by the collar, Ryan's warning obliterated from his mind. "Don't you ever *dare*—"

"You trying to tell me this is something other than a media-palatable land grab? Don't waste your breath, Garrison. You know as well as I do that this deal suits *nobody* but you. You screwed her in more ways than one."

Alex's fist clenched. He wanted nothing more than to smash the self-satisfied smirk from Murdoch's face.

Trouble was, Murdoch was right.

Alex had screwed Emma. He'd used her, and

he'd lied to her. And what he'd won was a half-billion-dollar property, a ridiculous prenup that forced her to stay with a man she probably hated, and half of her business, when she could have bailed herself out financially if he'd only been honest with her.

He got what he'd set out to win. But he'd lost so much more in the process.

He slowly let Murdoch go, then sank back into his chair.

How exactly was he different than Murdoch, or even David for that matter? If Alex could go back in time, he'd tell Emma all about Kayven Island, wait for her to sell it, then romance her, no strings attached.

He almost laughed at the absurdity.

He wanted Emma more than he wanted the island, more than he wanted the money, more than he wanted anything, really. All he wanted was for Emma to redecorate his house so they could throw party after party and fill that mausoleum with life and laughter.

Well, he couldn't have that. Not anymore. But he didn't have to take Emma down with him.

He took a deep breath. "I'll sell it to you," he said to Murdoch.

"Not with free staffing, you won't."

"I'll sell it to you for double the agreed-upon price, no staffing, no other conditions."

Murdoch's eyes narrowed.

"That's the only offer I'm making," said Alex. "Take it or leave it."

He could give Emma the money, and give her back McKinley. She could bail the company out of debt, and his partners… Well, his partners would just have to learn to live with it. Worst they could do is gang up and fire him as CEO.

If they did, he'd live with it. Just as long as he'd done right by Emma.

After two days and four pints of caramel pecan dream, Emma swore to herself that she was through with grieving. She had lost, and Alex had won. And that's the way it happened in the big bad world.

At least she still had half her company. And she and Katie could still work toward buying him out. Someday, anyway. For now, he was her partner. She wouldn't allow herself to think of him as anything more.

She wouldn't divorce him, but she wouldn't live with him either. If he wanted to talk to her, he could do it at the office. Her door was always open to all of her business associates.

An associate.

Yes. She liked that term.

In fact, she almost looked forward to seeing him again. She wanted him to know she was over him, that she'd picked herself up, learned from the experience and carried on.

Katie appeared in the bedroom doorway.

"This just came for you," she said, entering the room, holding out a cardboard envelope.

"From downstairs?" asked Emma, coming briskly to her feet. It was time to get back down to the office anyway.

"Crosstown courier," said Katie.

Emma took the envelope and tugged on the tab. The Garrison offices return address jumped out, but she refused to let it rattle her. There'd be plenty of correspondence between her and Alex from here on in. She could handle it.

"What is it?" asked Katie as Emma's gaze focused on the letter.

Emma read the brief paragraphs then shook her head and started over again.

"What?" Katie repeated.

The message finally sorted itself into some kind of order inside Emma's brain. "He sold Kayven Island."

"*What?*"

Emma squeezed her eyes shut, then refocused on the bank draft clipped to the top of the letter. "Alex sold Kayven Island to Murdoch."

Katie moved closer. "I thought the whole point was to *not* sell Kayven Island to Murdoch. How much…" She peered over Emma's shoulder. "Holy *crap!*"

Katie tried to read the letter, but Emma's hand was shaking too hard. So Katie had to still it.

"He's giving it back?" asked Katie.

Emma reread the words. "He says we should use Murdoch's money—" Her gaze went involuntarily to the amount on the bank draft. Holy crap indeed. "—to pay off McKinley's debts. And then it's ours. A hundred percent. Free and clear."

"He's tearing up the prenup," said Katie as she continued reading. "What's this about redecorating his house?"

"It's a joke." Emma laughed weakly. "When we were goofing around on Kayven…" When they were goofing around on Kayven, all her dreams were coming true. She'd dared to hope. Now, her eyes stung with the need to give him another chance. Was Alex truly that sweet, funny, sexy man? Or was that man a fraud, contrived to distract her? And which one of them had written the letter.

How would she ever know for sure?

Katie stared at her. "You do know what this means?"

Emma nodded. It definitely meant one thing. "We own our company again."

Katie elbowed her in the arm. "It means he wants you to *redecorate his house.*"

Emma scrambled to keep her emotions out of it. She had to thank logically. "That was just a joke."

"A joke? A guy who's giving up this many million dollars doesn't make jokes for the sake of a joke. He wants you. He probably loves you."

"Then why is he tearing up the prenup? Without the prenup, I can divorce him." Her voice caught. "He wants me to divorce him."

Katie squealed in frustration. "He wants you to come to him. Because you *want* to. Without coercion. He gave you back your money." She stared at the draft. "And *then* some. He gave you your freedom. But at the same time he mentions redecorating? Earth to Emma."

Emma's mouth went dry, and her heart thudded in her chest. Could Katie be right? Did she have the guts to find out?

"Go to him," said Katie. "Thank him. *Redecorate* him for God's sake. And do it now."

Emma bit her bottom lip. She wanted this, desperately wanted this. But if Katie was wrong… "You really think—"

"Go! I'm going to the bank." Katie glanced down again. "Holy crap."

Emma swung the mansion's big oak door wide open and strode into the foyer.

"Mrs. Garrison. So good to see you."

"Good to see you, too, Mrs. Nash. Is Alex in?"

If she was wrong, Emma had already decided

to pretend it was all a joke. She'd pretend she'd only stopped by to thank him for his gentlemanly, yet fair, behavior. And the rest was just a big joke.

No hard feelings. No harm done.

Mrs. Nash stepped back, a wry smile on her lips. "He's out back. Oh, have you had lunch? I can bring out some tea or sandwiches? Philippe has this great—"

"Philippe is here?"

Mrs. Nash laughed, and her cheeks turned slightly pink. "Oh, no. Of course not. Not at the moment."

Despite herself, Emma grinned. "Is it fair to say he'd be willing to help with future parties?"

Mrs. Nash nodded. "I think that would be fair to say."

Okay. That was a happy outcome.

Emma would cling to that.

She made her way past Hamilton and the other Garrison portraits, her chest tightening and her pulse increasing.

Oh, please let Katie be right.

Emma cut through the breakfast room, onto the deck, then down the stairs to the pool.

Alex was at an umbrella table, reading the *Times*. He glanced up at the sound of her footsteps.

"Emma." He was on his feet in an instant.

She slowed to a stop in front of him, not sure any more what she should say. The moment took on a surrealistic quality and her bravado evaporated. "Hello, Alex."

The sea breeze whispered through the aspen trees while they stared at each other.

"You got my letter?" he finally asked, his expression giving nothing away.

Emma nodded stiffly. "Thank you."

He moved forward. "It was just business, you know."

Her heart sank slowly in her chest, her palm going slick against the briefcase. He wasn't going to buy that it was a joke. This was definitely going to be embarrassing. "I know."

"It was nothing personal."

She flinched. "Of course not."

"I knew what I knew, and you knew what you knew, and I made the best deal possible for my company."

She'd been a fool to come here. A fool to think… "So you said."

"There was no reason to tell you up front." He gave a harsh laugh. "A guy wouldn't get very far telling his competition his secrets, would he?"

"Right." She'd only hoped she could get out of here in time. "Well, I just—"

"But then…" Alex's tone softened, and the harsh slate look went out of his eyes. "Then I proposed to you. And maybe, maybe that was when the rules changed."

Emma stood frozen to the ground.

"And then I married you. And that definitely meant the rules had changed. And then…" He took her left hand, rubbing his thumb over the Tudor diamond. "Then I fell in love with you, and any right I'd ever had to treat you as a business adversary was gone."

The aspen trees rustled into the silence.

"Emma?"

She couldn't help smiling. It was going to be okay. It was really going to be okay. "You fell in love with me?"

"Yeah, I fell in love with you. What did you think I meant by 'saying it'?"

"That you were in love with me." At least that was how it had seemed in the moment.

"Damn straight."

"Or that it might only be part of the game." She had to admit, the thought had crossed her mind.

"You thought our time on the beach was a game?"

She shook her head, her chest tightening with joy. "No. Not the beach."

On the beach, she'd believed him. On the beach, she'd dared to hope they were starting a glorious life together. Kind of like she did now.

"The beach was real," he rumbled. "That beach was the most real moment of my life."

Emma's, too. Oh, Emma's, too. She felt moisture heat the insides of her eyelids.

"I love you, Emma," Alex whispered, lifting her hand to place a gentle kiss on her knuckles.

Her mouth curved into a relieved smile.

Alex loved her.

He *loved* her.

"Well?" he asked.

"What?"

"Do I have to make you say it?"

She gazed into his dark eyes, her smile turning impish. "Yeah."

"Later," he whispered with a nod to where Mrs. Nash emerged onto the deck. A stream of people trailed out behind her.

"Hello?" Alex's brow shot up.

"I hope Mrs. Nash doesn't have anything against Italian decorators," said Emma, as the troop rounded the sun umbrella.

There was an unmistakable grin in Alex's voice. "We're redecorating?"

"I took a chance," she admitted. "And I mentioned your name. They have swatches and flooring samples."

He chuckled and he shook his head. "In that case, you don't have to say it."

"Why not?"

He took the case from her hand. "Because you just proved it."

She playfully elbowed him in the ribs. "Oh, make me say it anyway."

Alex leaned down and kissed her mouth. It was a warm, tender kiss, full of love, full of hope, full of the promise of a lifetime.

"I love you," she whispered on a sigh.

He drew back only slightly. "See, that was way too easy."

She leaned her cheek against his chest, enjoying the feel of his strong arms around her. "When it comes to you," she crooned, "I'm always easy."

He snorted his disbelief. But his fingertips sent a different message, trailing lightly along her spine. "You know, we have a honeymoon to finish."

"I guess we do."

"The *Island Countess* leaves for Fiji tonight." He paused. "And I know a guy who can get us a suite."

She pulled back. "I've seen those suites. They're fabulous."

"I have fond memories of them myself."

By the time the *Island Countess* blew her horn and pulled away from the dock, Emma was naked and wrapped tight in Alex's arms. The sounds of the late-night launch party tinkled up from the aft sundeck pool.

She buried her face in the crook of Alex's neck and inhaled his masculine scent. "I love you," she sighed.

He kissed the top of her head. "Wonder what else I can make you do."

"Pretty much anything at the moment. As long as it doesn't require movement. Or thinking. Or staying awake, actually." She stifled a yawn.

"You hungry?"

She shook her head. "Not hungry."

"Thirsty?"

"I'm fully satisfied, thank you."

He chuckled against her hair. "That's what I like to hear from my wife."

She smiled.

The phone on the bedside rang.

"Uh-oh," she said.

"Nothing else can go wrong," he assured her. Then he picked it up. "Garrison here."

He listened for a moment. "So it's done?"

Another pause.

"It'll be public?"

Emma came up on her elbow to watch his expression.

He smiled. "Yeah. Thanks. I owe you one."

Then he hung up the phone.

She waited.

"So, who was it?" she asked.

Alex closed his eyes. "Nathaniel."

"Oh." She waited again. "Well?"

He opened one eye. "What?"

"Is it a secret?"

"No." He opened the other eye and a smug grin took over his face. "Turns out, when the local government heard Kessex Cruise Lines had some concerns with the Kayven Island dock, they decided to move it."

Emma sat up. "What?"

"To another island, about five hundred miles east."

"You didn't."

"I didn't do a thing."

Emma leaned in closer, pasting Alex with an openly skeptical look. "You just told Nathaniel you owed him."

"Oh, that." Alex wave a hand. "That was—" He grinned. "Yeah. I did it. Murdoch needed to learn not to mess with us."

Emma tried hard not to be happy about getting revenge. "Remind *me* not to mess with you."

Alex pulled her into a hug. "You, woman, can mess with me any old time you like."

She pulled back and batted her eyelashes. "Like now?"

"I thought you were tired."

"I changed my mind. Apparently you vengeful types turn me on."

He slipped his hand across her hip and snuggled her up tight against his body. "Better not be any other vengeful types onboard."

"Better keep a close eye on me. Just in case."

He kissed her then. "You bet I will." Then he drew back. "By the way. I made an investment on behalf of McKinley."

She studied his eyes. "What did you do?"

"Bought a piece of property. Little bed-and-breakfast on Tannis Island. That's about five hundred miles east of Kayven. Not much to look at really. But I think it's going to be extremely valuable by the end of the week."

Emma fought a smile of astonishment. "You didn't."

His eyes softened, and he gazed at her with a love that sizzled through every fiber of her being. "You can bet I did."

* * * * *